Unveiling Bonds

JOURNEYS OF LOVE, TRUTH AND FAMILY

N. Sneha Vasundara

INDIA • SINGAPORE • MALAYSIA

ISBN 979-8-89067-945-1

About Author

Our Author Sneha Vasundara's life, rooted in Visakhapatnam, is a vivid tapestry woven with determination and ardor. Her initial foray into the world of dentistry showcased her innate ability to merge skill with compassion, lighting up countless faces with restored smiles. Sneha's gentle touch and genuine rapport with her patients are a testament to her unwavering commitment to making a difference.

However, life's unpredictable paths led Sneha from the dental chair to Writing. she plunged into the literature world, applying the same fervor and dedication she once reserved for her patients. While the realms of dentistry and literature might seem poles apart, Sneha's journey is proof that with grit, any domain can be mastered.

Sneha's heart beats loudest for her family. As a doting wife and mother of two, she elegantly balances work and home, ensuring her abode in Visakhapatnam resonates with warmth and joy. Her garden, a living tribute to her adoration for nature, offers her a sanctuary of peace and a profound bond with the earth.

When the city sleeps and serenity envelops Visakhapatnam, Sneha delves into the literary world, letting riveting tales whisk her away. This affection for literature, melded with her diverse life experiences, inspires her novels.

The vibrant characters she conjures, the intricate worlds she designs, all echo fragments of her own expedition.

Diving into Sneha's latest masterpiece isn't just about exploring a narrative; it's an invitation to experience a segment of her soul. Embracing roles from a dentist and MBA graduate to a devoted mother and nature enthusiast, Sneha Vasundara's tale, much like her novels, celebrates the myriad hues of life's grand journey.

Foreword

In the realm of storytelling, don't we all seek tales that echo our own experiences? Stories that make us feel and that take us on a journey across emotions, places, and lives "Unveiling Bonds: Journeys of Love, Truth, and Family" is one such tale, and it feels like its author has painted each word directly from the palette of her own life.

As I dug into this book, it wasn't just characters I met but also parts of the author herself. It's fascinating how she brings her unique experiences to bear. Through her tales, I felt the love of her family, her commitment to her work, and her appreciation for the beauty around us.

The beauty of this book is its authenticity. As you read, you don't just connect with the characters but with the author too. It's a journey into human emotions, decisions, and the little moments that make our lives worth living. Think of it like a canvas – every story, every emotion, paints a part of a bigger picture, capturing the essence of life.

As you turn the pages of "Unveiling Bonds: Journeys of Love, Truth, and Family," embrace the emotions and memories they bring. Here, you'll not just find stories but also the heartbeat of an author who brings her world to us in vivid colors.

I hope you find as much joy, introspection, and connection in this book as I did. Here's to the stories we live and the stories we tell.

Warm regards,

– Rajendra Kumar Kalla
Head of Product – Fitterfly
B.Tech – IITR | MBA – ISB

Preface

Some stories stand out among the many strands of human destiny, where destinies are intertwined and roads meet, as extraordinary and truly exceptional. Two couples are the subject of this tale. This story traces the journey of two couples whose lives were profoundly impacted by love, care, fate, and the untried paths they dared to travel.

As the narrator of their shared journey, I have seen how their emotions have fluctuated, as well as the obstacles that have tried their relationships and the joyful moments.

As the tale unravels, you will be drawn into the lives of Saraswati, Rishi, Sanjay, and Sindhuja. You will travel with these couples as they travel from the frantic city streets to the serene embrace of nature. They learned that love is not a destination but a transformative force that shapes and molds the very essence of who we are through laughter and tears, times of joy and pain.

What starts out as a desire for vengeance develops into a relentless search for the truth, which is hidden beneath multiple layers of lies and half-truths.

In the heart of this narrative lies a stirring exploration of the human psyche – how love and hate can blend into a tumultuous mixture. How seeking the truth can lead to unexpected discoveries

Dear reader, May you discover echoes of your own struggles and victories as you set out on this varied pursuit through the interwoven fabric of retribution and revelation. May you examine the lines between right and wrong, justice and retaliation, and, in the end, may you come to understand that the search for the truth is a path that leads to a more in-depth comprehension of ourselves and the intricate relationships that shape our lives.

Lots of Love,

– N. Sneha Vasundara

Acknowledgements

I am incredibly grateful to the people listed below who have helped me along the way, because writing a book is an expedition that is never undertaken alone.

Thank you my dear parents and my dear partner Dr. Kalyan Chakravarthy for your support and encouragement.

To Rajendra Kumar Kalla, my very best friend, who has always believed in my ability to write and has supported and encouraged me.

My sincere gratitude to my dear friend Manoj Kumar Padisetty for patiently listening to my plot twists and character conflicts

I became a bookworm thanks to my dear uncle P. Vijay Kumar, who is also my go-to source for books, and he has always provided me with advice.

To my beta reader, Rohith Sanjeev, who pointed out the plot holes and celebrated and appreciated my triumphs.

To Notion Press Publications, whose years of experience and direction have guided me through the intricate and challenging world of publishing.

Finally, I want to express my gratitude to the readers who will soon travel on this adventure with my characters for their curiosity and willingness.

With gratitude,

– N. Sneha Vasundara

When are you getting married? Has anyone asked you yet? My bad. Why wouldn't anyone ask anyone? In my opinion, no one is exceptional at receiving such inane questions from mankind. People both inside and outside your habitat make you feel reckless and irresponsible in your own life because you haven't married yet.

Because we do not pay taxes for what we say and the right to speak is unquestionably a fundamental right in our country, they simply make you a scapegoat by accusing you of being single and ignoring your fervent, vociferous opinions.

What baffles me is why so many people fail to understand the obvious fact that marriage is only a significant phase or part of life, not the rigid reason for our entire existence on this planet, and that the prime concern for marriage is the couple who are willing to be wed, and the rest comes next, but in most cases, the rest comes first. Some people find great fulfillment and happiness in marriage, while others do not. Ultimately, the importance of marriage in an individual's life is a matter of personal choice and perspective.

When it comes to girls, she finds it absurd to be in a position where you essentially know how to shut them up while also having the restraint to avoid the unintended consequence. Most of them will be married despite not being prepared for a lifetime commitment or willing to make sacrifices for no reward.

She is frequently questioned about her marriage, regardless of her age, willingness, or interests. If she chooses to marry later, but after the age of 25, she and her family are tittle – tattled about her marriage in the community.

In this case, we are talking about the girl's upcoming wedding once she completes her education. However, in other instances, the predicament of our sisters has gotten worse, made worse by the fact that some nations have categorically banned women from entering educational resource centers. I believe the discussion is heading somewhere and may result in controversies, so let us return to our original point and concern.

Fortunately, there are few Indian families that believe that education, career, and marriage are all equally important for a balanced life. Just like a balanced diet, we should be more focused on and prioritize segments like self care, relationships, work, etc. of the balanced life pyramid. Slowly but steadily, ideas and behaviors are evolving to support and normalize girls' aspirations. Despite how slight the change is, it's still a change.

Saraswati's situation deviates from how most Indian families view and approach marriage. Her family places a high value on education, and in fact, they are named after the goddess of learning and wisdom, Saraswathi. The traditionalists give their children names that honor the gods and goddesses or their ancestors. Please accept my apologies, Mataji, and respected elders.

Since the start of her relationship with books, from kindergarten through post-graduation, her family has played a crucial role in ensuring that every stage of education succeeds with good grades, and she never let down her parents, who, being all rounder, made all and sundry triumphantly happy.

This year marks her 27th birthday, and until today, no one in the house had mentioned a wedding or shown a green flag. She was always accompanied wherever she went and whenever she wanted to. Saraswati goes to cafes, bars, or out with pals, but there are strict restrictions on dating boys. She had never previously considered or been in a relationship. But, yeah, sometimes when she sees her friends' instant love affairs with boys, their maddening dramas, their daily instant breakups, and their equally quick reconciliations, she feels rescued from all these.

Saraswati, on her recent birthday, was given a gift by Mr. Mukesh, Saru's father, who declared that now she could date, so finally he has flown the green flag, though conditions are applied.

Saraswati is beautiful, intelligent, blossoming, single, and earning rupees as an interior designer in her homeland compared to her cousins, who are earning pounds in other states after leaving everything and living away from family, and she still makes a lot of money, especially as the only girl among her cousins not under the shade of her parents' support.

As I am talking about and providing information about her, you all must have assumed by now that this tale revolves around Saraswati, known affectionately as Saru. She triumphs over unexpected challenges, enduring unforeseen and unthinkable turns and twists, all while protecting both herself and her family. Amidst this journey of hers, she also experiences puppy love and the weighty emotion of love, and the tale probes how destiny alters her surname and the individual with whom she shares a transformative connection.

The month of June marked the beginning of the monsoon season in India, and Saturday evening welcomed the vibe of the weekend and relaxation mode. The air is cool and breezy, and the dark sky obscures the stars. The thick, dark clouds that hover above make the evening more pleasant.

Electrical currents and lightning strikes added to the dense blanket of dark clouds. The outcome was a thunderstorm; the larger and heavier crystals in the clouds began to fall and take the form of rain, but the glass pillars kept the balcony's wooden floor from absorbing the moisture. The birds flew, stopped on the house's eaves, and sought shelter, tucking their heads under the bright feathery plumes.

Mr. Mukesh: Would you call Rishi and tell them to return home because they took Max for a walk in the park and I attempted to call both but neither answered, and now my phone battery is flat?

Mr. Srinivas: It's possible that they both left their phones in the car. The ticking hands of the clock will lose their grip on the passing hours and days as they both engage in tireless and nonstop chatter. No matter if they dwell in the same abode. From sharing meals to grappling with chores, these two are glued, destined to entertain and bemuse one another every minute. Whether it's discussing the shrewd strategies behind the actions of our honorable prime minister while brushing their teeth or discussing the mysteries of history over a plate of idli, now the rain was so heavy that by the time they got back to the car, they'd be completely soaked."

Mr. Mukesh: Ha ha, no doubt at all; their bond is so special. Due to the current inclement weather, especially Saru, is the source of all my worries. She is more prone to catching colds after getting wet in the rain. Still today, like a young child, she is resistant to taking her medications, and she annoys us with her tantrums and acts out in ways that can be disruptive and upset the entire environment of the house.

Mr. Srinivas: I understand; don't fret over much, and I see why you are taking trips to the balcony every two minutes. Cool off, Mukesh. She is no longer a child; she is an adult capable of caring for herself, and she will be fine with Rishi by her side, who will not let her get wet, and I know my son is very caring towards all of us, especially Saru.

Mr. Mukesh: Yes, Srinivas, our children have been bonded since the day they were born, and they look out for one another.

Mr. Mukesh and Mr. Srinivas advanced to the balcony, gathered their chairs, and dragged them to the other side of the balcony to avoid the raindrops that were falling near the edge of the glass slabs.

Leo is pacing front and back near the balcony door, bowing and inviting Mr. Mukesh and Mr. Srinivas to play with him, possibly looking out and inside the house for someone to come and take him outside.

Mr. Mukesh: These kids took Max and left Leo.

This little one has no company and is too young to go on outings or to parks, so he must be bored.

Mr. Srinivas: Yes, it is pitiful that Max was taken away, and now Leo is left alone without his playmate. Anyway, soon three of them will arrive home, and what are the weekend plans? Any updates on meeting with these budding startups?

Mr. Mukesh: I haven't received any new emails as of yet, but I did send the PR to them. Hopefully, tomorrow will bring news of our interest, and we will certainly proceed with the new project. Isn't it tempting to eat hot fritters during the first monsoon rain?

Mr. Srinivas: Well, then let's wait for tomorrow for good news to fill our ears, and I'm on a diet, specifically the Pegan diet, so a big no.

Mr. Mukesh: Last time you mentioned some sort of Mediterranean diet, when did you shift to this? You were fortunate, Srinivas, to frequently enjoy different cuisines without entering hotels.

Mr. Srinivas: Not funny; everyone was bantering with me about my diets; now that you have joined the fray, you did not spare me either. You must be acquainted with your sweet sister, Roja, who is always trying out all the latest food diets on me as a guinea pig in the research lab.

Mr. Mukesh: Haha, I feel sorry for you; I can't get you off these diets because my hands are tied with sisterly love.

Mr. Srinivas: Ah, I knew you'd say that. The problem was that I was closing my eyes with dedication, ticking off the list of favorite items on the agenda paper that I had to leave until this diet ends, but marble cake, tiramisu, chocolate fudge, peanut and sesame clusters, and regular munchers—I couldn't seem to get away from them. With great effort, I would divert my thoughts away from marble cake, but then I'd be thinking of tiramisu, and so on.

Mr. Mukesh: Shake off cravings; it's a never ending cycle of temptations. It's a tough situation to be in, but hopefully you can find a way to satisfy the cravings without breaking the diet.

Mr. Srinivas: Everybody tells me I need to overcome cravings, but no one ever seems to have any suggestions for how to do it without causing discomfort to my taste buds.

Mr. Mukesh: Ha ha. That's the simplest advice anyone could give you, and I'd also advise you to simply shake your head off when food is put in front of you.

Receiving this comment, Mr. Srinivas erupted into belly laughs, and Mr. Mukesh joined in. Leo barked, waggled his tail, and jumped up and down when he saw both of them. Mrs. Sharmila enters the balcony, draped in a pinkish-orange luxurious silk fabric, adorned with minimal sequins, and wearing elegant jewelry, carrying a plate of hot fritters with green mint and sweet tamarind chutneys, and says, "Who would like to indulge in some hot and crispy fritters in the rain and relaxing atmosphere?"

Mr. Mukesh: I must say, Sharmila, that you read my mind so perfectly when myself and your brother were both talking about some hot, crispy onion pakodas, and now you are with them.

Mrs. Sharmila: Yeah, Mukesh, my love, after thirty years of marriage, you still think I can't read and anticipate your every desire? and presented the fritters on plates with a playful smile.

Mr. Srinivas: Don't serve these to me, as they're hot, crispy, and appetizing. Please take them away from my sight, Sharmila, or else I'll start with one and consume all the fritters served, and then I'll be wearing a penitent expression.

Mrs. Sharmila: I'll be sitting here watching you, Anna, so just have some; at the very least, taste them.

Mr. Srinivas: If you look at my belly, you'll notice that it has grown by two inches more in circumference, and if Roja finds out, it's no surprise that she'll put me on a leaf diet. I envision myself eating leaves while dangling from a tree branch, just like the Moroccan goat that climbs trees. However, I wouldn't put myself at risk of starving by only eating leaves.

Mr. Mukesh: Roja is incredibly dedicated when it comes to maintaining a healthy weight. She consistently makes smart choices about what is consumed, and she does everything to keep your weight down.

Ms. Sharmila: chuckled and remarked that fritters are the spice of life, and indulging in a few fritters every once in a while wouldn't cause any trouble. In fact, it might even bring a little extra joy and deliciousness to our lives.

Mr. Srinivas: Indulging in some fritters, mmm, is so gratifying, and a hot cup of chai would be perfect for this beautiful weather.

Mrs. Sharmila: I knew you'd say it, so here I am with a pot of steaming hot masala chai.

Mrs. Sharmila poured into the cups after speaking. Mr. Mukesh rubbed his hands together, generating heat that stimulated his thermoreceptors and made him feel warm. He then picked up a cup of chai from the table, sipped it, selected a fritter, chewed and savored it for a while, and suggested that more carrom seeds be added to the pakoda. The helper, Sita, was called in, and Mrs. Mukesh instructed her to add a spoonful of carrom seeds to the onion pakodas for the subsequent batch and not add much; the fritters might taste bitter.

Sita nodded and left for the kitchen.

Mr. Srinivas: The fritters taste perfect to me.

I must admit that my sister Sharmila, who wields magic in her cooking, is partly to blame for my size.

Mr. Mukesh: Beloved brother-in – law, I humbly ask you to share your honest comments with us.

Mr. Srinivas: He he, Dear Sharmila, onion pakodas are tasty but briny.

Mrs. Sharmila: Anna, I just had some, and the taste is fine. A few minutes ago, you praised me for my cooking, and now you are teasing me and taking Mukesh's side.

Mr. Srinivas: Okay, okay, if you compensate, I don't mind retracting my remarks about fritters.

Mrs.Sharmila: Ah, then, how about your favorite dinner food tonight? And any cravings can be satisfied, Anna.

Mr. Srinivas: Well, this compensation sounds manageable, and I told you I couldn't stop at just tasting, so I'm gobbling up fritters.

Dressed in her co-ords workout attire, Mrs.Roja was all set to take an evening walk, but she was waiting for the rain to stop. When she reached the balcony, she noticed that they were enjoying and eating fritters; eventually, she joined and picked a delectable fritter to relish and remarked, "It's just perfect and delicious."

Mr. Mukesh: Oh, Roja. Me and Srinivas were really letting loose, gossiping about your sister-in-law's cooking skills and relishing the fritters.

Mrs. Roja: Sharmila, I've got this situation covered, like a blanket on a cold night. I won't let anything happen that would make you turn red as a tomato. You two have officially run out of jokes to tell one another, so you both are aiming for Sharmila.

Mr. Srinivas: As all four of us are here, everyone is in high spirits and full of cheer. I have significant news to share and have been holding onto it for the right moment. Mr. Murthy Ji spoke about his daughters' marriage to our Rishi, and they are ready for marriage anytime this year.

Mr. Sharmila: Oh, my goodness, congratulations! So, our Rishi will soon tie the knot.

Mr. Mukesh: This is fantastic news. Sharmila, please fetch the sweets. The moment has come for us to rejoice and revel in celebration of this phenomenal occasion.

Everyone was overjoyed with the news, and as part of it, Mr. Srinivas mentioned that he spoke with Pandit Ji, who advised them to hold Rishi's engagement ceremony in the upcoming month of Sravanam. Given that this is the first wedding in their family following their own, Mr. Mukesh expressed his delight and said that it should be a magnificent celebration. Mrs. Sharmila shared her excitement and said that they would make sure that the celebrations were grand and spectacular.

Mr. Srinivas: Yeah, definitely. Mukesh, I totally forgot about the evening's meeting, which was scheduled for 6.30; shouldn't we start now?

Mr. Mukesh: Yes, surprisingly. I, too, forgot about the meeting. We've both been working hard to get this meeting with the delegates scheduled. Thank you for reminding me about the meeting, Srinivas, which had slipped my mind, and please also call for assistance in keeping the laptop bag and other necessary items in the car.

Mr. Srinivas: Sharmila, prior to my departure, I want to say it again to you as a reminder that you don't forget to whip up something delicious in the kitchen; your culinary abilities are impressive, and they are on par with the exceptional cooking abilities of our dear mother.

Mrs. Sharmila: Haha, well, that's huge. I see my culinary skills have finally impressed you, my dear sweet brother, and now I'll have to start practicing my world's best cook acceptance speech. And next time, don't change your reviews to support my husband.

Mr. Srinivas and Mr. Mukesh looked at Mrs. Sharmila, and they both laughed at her words.

Mrs. Roja: Sharmila, don't pamper your beloved brother with too many carbs, or he will turn into a noddle.

Mrs. Sharmila and Mrs. Roja chortled and waved off their husbands and went back to their kitchen station and their conversations.

Mrs. Sharmila: Life is too short to be counting carbs all the time; sometimes you just have to say, "Carbs be damned!" and indulge in some favorite and comfort foods. Did you see Anna? He is positively beaming over Rishi's engagement, and of course, for this reason, he is deserving of a delectable sweet treat.

Mrs. Roja: That makes sense. I'll remember that. But balance it out with some healthy choices.

Mrs. Sharmila: Noted, but all of a sudden, what has caused your energy to dissipate, and why did you replace a bright face with a more neutral outlook? Is your concern regarding my brother's diet, or is there a different issue at hand? Don't hide from me, though. I can tell from the expression on your face that it's like the tannin squeezed out of the clothes, leaving a brown hue.

Mrs. Roja: I am good. Thank you for noticing. I just have a lot weighing on my mind currently.

Mrs. Sharmila: Oh, Roja. Now quit the drama of being too formal and polite; cut to the chase.

Mrs. Roja: Huh. It's not about Srinivas' diet or health but rather something else, but I am faring well, Sharmila.

Mrs. Sharmila: Uff, this is the last time I'm asking you. Are you telling me or not?

Mrs. Roja: Okay, I must admit that Sindhuja's readiness to wed Rishi still astounds me. It's evident that they both attended the same school. However, when the school reached out to all of its alumni, their paths crossed, and she developed feelings for him and proposed to him. How they could both understand and love each other so deeply in just a few days is the most enigmatic of all. Rishi accepted her and decided to be together through the events as they transpired. I have a strong suspicion that he is concealing something.

Mrs. Sharmila: Hey, Roja, don't sweat it. I believe they have exchanged hearts and discussed ideas and future plans. Take comfort in the fact that we are at least informed. Nowadays, millennials prefer to get married in secret and leave the poor family folks out of it, which is becoming a trend. I can't believe they are not inviting their own parents to their wedding. It's just disrespectful and shows a lack of appreciation for everything parents have done for their children. Of course, I meant others; Rishi would never do something like this to us. Recall that my childhood friend Radha was recently admitted to the hospital, and when I went to see her, she told me that her son, who had visited Canada last year and had surprised everyone by introducing his wife to everyone via video call, was the reason for the elevated artery pressure.

Mrs. Roja: What are you saying? I don't want to spend every hour in a hospital getting poked and allowing tiny, sharp needles to pierce my skin deeply while also having to endure torturous, continuous beeps that make you feel as though you are at the gate of death.

Mrs. Sharmila: You are unbelievable, Roja; you have extracted this from what I told you. Huh…

Mrs. Roja: Sharmila, despite the enlightening insights, I appreciate what Rishi and Sindhuja did to move their relationship forward, but I still have anxiety about their marriage because of some pesky and bothersome thoughts.

Mrs. Sharmila: Then it's time for a straightforward and sincere talk with him, but avoid imposing your opinions on him; instead, make an effort to listen to him attentively, demonstrate that you understand his point of view, and just show empathy for his perspective. It might release your burden.

Mrs. Roja: Agh, I had an open and sincere conversation with him, but unfortunately it didn't yield the desired results, and he remained his usual upbeat self, like ever.

Mrs. Sharmila: That sounds good to me; there is no need to worry if clarification dispels the doubts, and it implies that our Rishi is thrilled to embark on a new journey in life with Sindhuja, who has a well-bred background, a good education, and polite manners.

Mrs. Roja: Nevertheless, my heart and mind are not yet fully convinced. I would definitely say again that he's not being transparent with us.

Mrs. Sharmila: Roja, you were overthinking and ended up with negative consequences. Don't ruminate on negative thoughts because it raises your stress levels. Moreover, marriage is still some time away, so he has time to ponder and reflect. I have faith in Rishi's judgment and believe that he will not engage in any actions that would lead to pain or difficulty for himself or us.

Mrs. Roja: It seems probable that you are correct in this matter, and I am keeping my fingers crossed that everything will be alright in the end.

Mrs. Sharmila: Well, now be upbeat and assist me in preparing my brother's favorite meal.

To please their family members' palates, Mrs. Sharmila and Mrs. Roja devoted a significant portion of the evening to crafting a culinary extravaganza. Mrs. Sharmila and Mrs. Roja always explored a wide range of flavors and techniques and experimented with ingredients to concoct a plethora of delectable dishes that would tantalize every palate. As the aromas of their culinary efforts wafted through the house, it evoked a sense of eagerness among the members of the family. As dinner was laid out on the table, every dish was a hit. Each dish was bursting with flavors and textures that left everyone at the table asking for more. Mrs. Sharmila and Mrs. Roja received a shower of compliments for their exceptional skills in crafting such a delightful meal. Later, when Rishi and Saru returned home from their fun-filled evening with Max, they joined the rest of the family for the feast, filling the already joyous atmosphere with more warmth and happiness. The elders made the decision to officially announce Rishi's engagement date and celebrate Saru's birthday in front of close family and friends.

The special day has arrived, Saru's birthday. The entrance was spectacular, and to the existing garden, many more plant pots were added. Both of the homes are exquisitely decorated while keeping it simple. Meticulous attention was given to every detail. At the entrance, a quirky and delightful display of trays full of lollipops, gummies, marshmallows, and sour candies awaited the guests. The idea was curated to evoke a playful and notable atmosphere, catering to the inner child in everyone. As she doesn't like the cake-cutting ceremony on the stage, given that it was her birthday, family members respect her wish.

When the time was right, Mr. Srinivas' couple made the announcement about Rishi's engagement. People were congratulating and blessing the family, and a few aunts circled each other, biting each other's ears.

Mrs. Ratna: The girl in the mustard lehenga is the bride, isn't she? And she is stunning.

Mrs. Lata: Gulping down some colorful water, Shh, Ratna, she's Saru, the only child of Mr. Mukesh and

Mrs. Sharmila, not the bride, but she is the birthday girl. The bride's family couldn't make it as they were in another country for a holiday.

Mrs. Ratna: Aw, they make a cute couple; why couldn't these two get married?

Mrs. Lata: Ah, good question. Earlier, we all felt the same way because they both shared a close upbringing. Contrary to popular belief, they have remained close cousins and best friends; they were born in the same year, lived in adjacent houses, and attended the same school. More than cousins, each of them has been the other's favorite.

Mrs. Ratna: Hmm, interesting, Lata. Speaking of decorations, someone has a keen eye for design, and these decorations really set the tone and mood for the occasion.

Mrs. Lata: In terms of the decorations and arrangements, Saru handled and managed everything while taking into account everyone's preferences, and the output was great. You may also be interested to know that, recently, she undertook the prestigious project of designing a five-star luxury hotel, which was a rousing and resounding success. Her extraordinary accomplishments at such a young age have garnered her the respect and admiration of prestigious clubs and organizations in various cities.

As the aunties engaged in their favorite pastime of exchanging juicy tidbits and rumors, they welcomed more of their comrades – in arms into the fold of rumor-mongering. Meanwhile, the uncles were lounging around, chilling, and soaking themselves in the delightful drama. It appeared as though a parallel universe of entertainment was taking place before their very eyes, with each group having a blast in its own special way.

Saru was spending some "me time" in the right corner of the large hall, completely oblivious to the flow of calories and engrossed in welcoming excess calories while sipping her own beverage and browsing the designs of blouses that would look great with a lehenga on Pinterest.

Saru could see the crowd of aunties approaching like sheep busting when the gates of the pen were opened, and she thought, "No doubt, these aunties were going to evaporate me with their illogical and irrelevant questions about my marriage," and she tried to slip out of place.

Saru was unlucky to catch Lalitha Aunty's attention, the most repulsive member. She was one of the rabble, and she was responsible for her son's lifetime of suffering as a result of forced marriage. She has the authority to control everyone and treats her daughter-in-law as an employee who obeys without question, much like an autocrat.

Hello there, Saru Beta! wished Mrs.Lalitha.

Saru: Greetings, Lalitha Aunty! How are things going for you?

Mrs. Laitha: Don't worry about me because I'm fantastic. You are such a smart and bubbly girl. You should think about your parents, especially since you don't have a brother to care for them. If you marry, your husband will be a son and take care of you all three.

Saru is beginning to lose her composure over Mrs. Lalitha's ridiculous and unrelated comments about her wedding. She suddenly became enraged and yelled, "Son!"

When she yelled, she caught the attention of a few people in the hall. Noticing it, Saru walked to the other corner of the room, grabbed a chair, and sat down to sip. She pondered, "How could my husband be a son to them?" as she sipped. "So she thinks I'm incapable of caring for my parents?" "I think Lalitha Aunty is insane, hasn't changed at all, and is now trying to ruin my life the same way she did her son's." Saru overheard, "My cousin has a handsome son who would make an excellent bridegroom for our Saraswathi."

Saru: What am I currently hearing? Oh God, my mom's walking buddy, Lata Aunty, is the one who experiments with different ingredients and cooking techniques in an effort to impress the people around her. Despite her redeeming qualities, I am only concerned with the outcomes that make the eaters sick.

Saru experienced a flush of irritation as another aunt joined the group and thought that "she needed to get out of here quickly or she'd be inundated with free advice from a slew of aunties." She threw a fake smile and said hello to Mrs. Lata and to the remaining aunties of the rabble.

Mrs. Lata: Hello, beta, How are you? As I mentioned, my nephew would be a perfect match for you. See, here is his photo.

Saru couldn't stop herself from looking at photographs of Lata's aunt's nephew, which she felt compelled to do. In the next moment, Mrs.Madhavi joins and talks about her nephew, who works for Google, and from nowhere, another aunty shows up and says, "What are you saying to her?" Don't poison her mind and heart. Don't derail her hopes. Don't break her dreams, and she advised Saru to grade her career.

As she is surrounded by these garrulous aunties and knows that if she stays with them for any longer, she will go insane, Saru pleads to God, Oh Lord, please, please pull me out of this circus.

Then Rishi shows up and rescues her from the circus while deftly dodging the aunts. She hugs Rishi for saving her. As they walked to the corridor, they both pulled out the sparsely placed extra chairs meant for the party and made themselves comfortable.

Saru: I desperately need a solution to stop them from consuming my brain like a pest.

Rishi: Those aunts' comments have inflamed you, and you are overanalyzing the situation and shouldn't be worried about their comments.

Saru: These aunties won't let me enjoy the party alone, and by the way, I should reprimand you for inviting all of your relatives, including their relatives, when you could have planned a small, sweet gathering instead.

Rishi: Oh, these aunts used to talk behind our backs at every gathering to which they were invited. Recall that at Reetu's baby shower, my mother and Lata Aunty got into a funny argument that quickly escalated into physical violence. I thank my dad for intervening before it turned into a physical altercation.

Saru: Yeah, who would forget that mini show? Well, it looks like a few of these aunts have quite the reputation for stirring up drama at family gatherings. It's like they have an automated answer machine on how to turn friendly meetings into WWE matches. Thank goodness your dad was there to prevent any flying-chairs and now that I've been saved, your marriage is still the elephant in the family room.

Rishi: Oh, instead of blaming and bothering me, thank me for rescuing you before they pull you into an argument and crush you. For your information, they are not only my relatives but also yours; kindly save this information in your hippocampus.

Saru: My gray cells have a greater ability to think than yours, so the hippocampus does not accept the unwanted information. So, I can't remember them all.

Rishi: Argh, it makes no sense to keep bugging each other for these aunts. I'm going to see my friends now that they've arrived after a trek and intend to tour the vicinity of the city. Would you like to come along?

Saru: Let's go, Mr. Savior; that sounds preferable to being crammed in between aunts.

Rishi: I want you to keep a few things in mind before I introduce my friends.

Saru: Oh, should I get some paper and a person to write them down?

Rishi: Sure, I can wait while you get them.

Saru smiles wittily at Rishi.

Rishi: Argh, pay attention now and stop making fun of me, or kindly do not be the source of someone else's amusement, and sometimes you rush into things without thinking and talking; don't be impetuous.

Saru: Ugh, Rishi, enough of that; now tell me the points to be highlighted.

Rishi: Okay, they're all single men looking for a partner, so they'll be hitting on you, making passes, and so on. They'll probably try to impress you with all their ridiculous antics and skills during this time, much like some birds do when they display brightly colored feathers and make rhythmic sounds to attract female birds, and they'll try to crack some dumb jokes. Once you've committed to laughing, you won't be able to tell the difference between good and bad jokes.

Saru: I must admit that it will be a very exciting and titillating evening with your friends, Rishi. Are there any handsome faces to hook up with?

Rishi: You obviously have high expectations, haha. By the way, who is saying this? Did you ever date a man? I was the only boy, the only man, who was allowed to communicate and interact with you from your girlhood to your young adulthood to your womanhood.

Saru: Oh, I know how unfair it is; however, things have changed; the universe has heard my prayers, and finally, my father has shown me the positive indicators, the green flag.

While I'm talking about dating freedom, I'm letting you go, relieving you of bodyguard duties. Moreover, I am now old enough and capable of making my own decisions, so please do not bring up unpleasant memories from the past and stop staring at me. The speech got finished, Rishi. haha... We're running late; let's go.

Rishi: I didn't anticipate this news at all. Consequently, how do you feel? Anyway, thanks for the update, Saru.

Saru: Rishi, what will you do with the update? I know the embarrassing look on your face; don't publicize this content on any social media sites and spare me from being embarrassed.

Rishi: Saru, you're so clever, and you get me so well. People should be aware of the latest news that you are ready to mingle in the human jungle.

Saru: huh..., Then consider this topic for tomorrow's headlines, so that later we can all scroll through the news channels.

Rishi: Nah, I just had a better idea to reach the largest possible audience: I would like to share the information among the aunties, and you are well aware of the speed and efficiency of these aunts' gossip communication networks, Saru.

Saru: I truly deny your contribution to tarnishing my reputation, and if you think about it, I will open your Pandora's box.

Rishi: Easy, my dear, don't go there, and I swear not to tease you anymore.

Saru: Good, Rishi. This is why you are the best in the world.

Rishi: chuckled. All right then, enough tugging at each other's ears; let's find you a match.

Saru and Rishi dashed down the stairs, past the comforting aromas of jalebis and rabdi from the temporary kitchen set up for a day of celebrations, but the desire to savor the sweet stopped Saru, and she paused for a brief moment, looking into Rishi's eyes.

Rishi closed his eyes and enunciated, "Resist temptation and maintain a polished appearance, so no weakening and succumbing to sweets." Saru felt adorable and amused when observing his enunciation, and she responded.

Saru: Oye, this one plate of jalebi won't turn you into a jalebi-shaped figure unless that's your goal.

Rishi: If my mother discovers this, she will force me to eat a plate full of colorful varieties of leaves and seeds for the next few days.

Saru: Oh, mama's boy, you're saying no and preventing the jalebis that are fried in ghee and soaked in sugar syrup from entering your mouth. Think of a hot, crispy, crunchy jalebi that has been liberally dipped in a bowl of creamy rabdi and eaten with tiny slices of pistachio, almond, and kesar. The combination of sugar syrup, jalebi, and rabdi, as well as the crackling sounds of jalebi, entices you to order another round.

Rishi: Saru, I refused to be diverted from my purpose. Please don't press me.

Saru: Uff. Then come over here and watch me eat my dear, handsome face haplessly.

Rishi wore an "Okay" facial expression that may be a mix of desire and self-control as he tried to resist the temptation to eat, and he sat near the front door, tapping his feet on the ground to kill time while Saru ate the first bowl of jalebis. Saru looked at Rishi and licked her rabdi-coated fingers, playfully teasing him.

Rishi: Saru, will you let me sit in peace? You were acting and instilling desire in me like a model in a commercial.

Saru: Haha, come here and join me in eating jalebis and fulfill your desire.

Rishi immediately lost control and ran over to Saru. He picked up an empty plate and asked the halwa wala for a serving, taking out a sizable piece of jalebi and devouring it like a child while liberally drizzling it with rabdi.

Saru: laughed loudly. You know, when the jalebis were all around you, I knew you couldn't sit still for more than a few seconds, and this reminds me of how you ran behind the ice popsicles on wheels in the streets.

Rishi's voice carried a hint of nostalgia as he remarked, "Ah, those beautiful days; I can't believe how quickly time flies. We had the best childhood together, filled with so many happy memories. But now things are changing, and soon I am about to embark on the journey of marriage."

Saru: Hey, are you feeling okay?

Rishi: Of course I am good, Saru.

Saru: My senses have been telling me that you have been under some stress and pressure for the past week. But as always, you tried to keep all of your emotions inside your good and compassionate heart and suppress them. Why are you upset?

Rishi: Saru, there is no such thing as bad, and everything is good.

Saru: I knew you'd say it: when people don't feel good or something bothers them, they stretch the truth or outright lie to make themselves appear better than they believe others perceive them to be.

Rishi: Oh, please save me from wasting my energy listening to your orations. You know what? You have the potential to become a well-liked orator who completely engages the audience during your speech, and your attractiveness will ensure that the class is full.

Saru: Uff, I appreciate the advice, but you won't change, so please don't come to me in the middle of the night to vent, and I will decline to allow you to sob on my shoulder.

Rishi glared down at her with a peevish expression on his face.

Rishi: I am all right. Okay, don't throw away your attitude. Are you thinking of continuing the silly squabbles with me while merrily finishing the jalebis from the forthcoming batch?

Saru: Not funny at all. Well, I don't have the mood to fight with you, so stick to the old plan.

Rishi remarked on her choice as a wise one, casting a glance over her shoulder, adjusting his goggles, and shuffled off towards the parking space. Saru followed him and took the passenger seat. She rummaged in her handbag and found a lip tint, which she applied to her lips and slightly rubbed on her cheeks. She asked Rishi to play her favorite playlist. Well, Rishi played a pasoori from Spotify.

After a few minutes of travel, they both reached the guest house where they were supposed to meet Rishi's friends. Rishi urged Saru to wait while he parked the car in the cellar, but she denied his words and walked to the guest house, as she wanted to use the bathroom.

Saru climbed the stairs to the first floor, which housed the living space. She pushed the bell button firmly, but no one showed up, and when she tried to knock, the door opened too little as it was unlocked.

She pushed the door open and called out; to her surprise, no one was seen or heard. Inside was illuminated and jet black, and the curtains were drawn, so there were no open windows that allowed sunlight to enter. She walked to the left side and switched on the lights, as she knew everything about the guest house because Rishi and Saru frequently visited and their families threw parties there often.

When Saru used the common restroom, she washed and dried her palms with the toilet paper and bent forward to throw the paper into the trash. As she stood up, someone pulled her hands back and placed a hand on her mouth.

Sanjay: Who are you? You look decent, and how could you break into someone's house to use the bathroom?

As Saru struggled to break free of him, she bit his hand. The man experienced pain and pulled his hand back. In a split second, Saru turned to face him; she was enthralled by his attractive face and shirtless, chiseled abs.

Sanjay: Hey, what are you looking at?

Saru suddenly snaps out of it and grabs the vase that was kept on the sink table as a decoration and yells, "You are shameless, walking around naked." And this is my guest house; how dare you hurt me?

Sanjay: Is it a new trend to break into and use other people's bathrooms, claim ownership of the property, and attack me like an animal?

Saru: Hey, you called me an animal? I am calling Rishi right now.

You're calling who? Sanjay questioned Saru.

"Rishi," Saru said, and she tossed the vase onto the floor an inch away from Sanjay as she writhed in agony. The vase breaking jolted Sanjay off the sofa, and they both broke into oral fights.

Sanjay: Hey, have you lost your mind? hmmm, wait... Yes, this is Rishi's place. Don't tell me; you're his cousin, Sarawathi.

Saru: exhaled heavily and said, Yes, I am. That is what I am attempting to convey to you, you moron.

Sanjay: Hey, hey, Saraswati, you should use your words carefully and wisely.

Saru: You don't give me that. Mr. Moron.

Sanjay: Damn, Look, Saraswati, I am Sanjay, Rishi's friend, and I feel awfully sorry for treating you like a burglar.

Hic, hic, hic.

Saru: I am having hiccups. Why are you staring at me? Will you let me die here? Hic.. hic.. Get me some water, you moron.

Sanjay clenched his teeth and hated it when she called him a moron and said, "You better call me Sanjay," and he hurtled to the refrigerator to search for water. The water bottles were empty. Sanjay reasoned that if he didn't give her water to drink, she'd call him a moron again, so he took the glass from the cabinet and poured the last of the vodka from the bottle into it, then handed her a little vodka.

Saru: Oh, my Buddha! Now he's tagging me as a burglar. What's going on with Rishi? How much time does he spend parking a car? I think he must be giving a special class on zoology to some uncle or aunt, whispering and saying, "Hey, moron, how much do you take to get a glass of water?"

Sanjay: Hey, I have a name, and I told you a few minutes ago.

Sanjay was annoyed and upset about Saru calling him a moron again. Instead of reacting impulsively, he decided he wanted to teach her a little discipline in the right usage of words and filled the glass with the last of the tap water.

Hic.. hic..

Sanjay handed the glass to Saru and told her to drink it. Saru snatched the glass from his grasp, gulped it down, and involuntarily spat the liquid on the ground out of reflex. Startled, she screamed, "What is this that you have given me?"

Sanjay: haha, Did you enjoy the mocktail of a moron?

Saru raged and looked around for something to throw at him. She found the decorative clock piece on the corner table and clutched it tightly. Sanjay noticed her dripping rage and tried to calm her down.

Sanjay: Saraswati, I apologize; could you put the vase back on the table?

Rishi: Hey everyone. Sorry, Saru, the uncle I met in the parking lot clung to me like a lizard on a wall and wouldn't let go. Eventually, however, I was able to get away from him. What happened? Why are you holding the vase in your hands?

Saru: You were probably glued to Uncle to educate him about the reptile family; don't blame him. Now you've arrived. Your friend, Moron, tagged me as a burglar.

Sanjay: Hey, Sarawati, Please refrain from calling me a fool. I told you my name is Sanjay.

Saru: Ah, fine, moron.

Rishi had a feeling something fishy was brewing between them before he arrived. Sanjay and Saru were babbling, ignoring Rishi's explanation for his lateness. He wanted to stop them, but they didn't seem to care about his words or presence. So he snatched the clock from Saru's grasp and tossed it to the floor. As the clock's clanging was so loud, Saru and Sanjay stopped moving their mouths, and the voices went off.

Saru: Have you lost your mind? What did you do, Rishi?

Sanjay: Man, relax your muscles. Relax, Rishi.

Rishi put a finger to his lips to silence them. Sanjay and Saru didn't move a muscle, and they kept their mouths silent, which were in full action for a while, and they behaved like the most obedient children in the class.

Rishi: Dear Saru, he is Sanjay, a good friend of mine with the most handsome face. Remember that before I joined our company, I was given a project to complete as experience; without his help, the project would not have been a success. Sanjay, this is Sarawati, my adorable and mischievous cousin.

As Rishi attempted to make a proper introduction, they both made careless and sloppy faces and threw fake smiles at each other. Knowing this, Rishi spotted a possible solution and made an instant story like Instant Maggie by saying, "He was receiving calls from home, so they might need his participation in performing some work." As he was leaving home, he said, "If you two are willing to wave a red flag to your crazy misreadings and misunderstandings about each other, we can leave to go home."

In a fit of anger, Saru maintained a stony silence while snatching the keys with her fingernails, showing assertive aggression towards Rishi. However, she fumed her way down to the parking area, seething with frustration. Sanjay was sorry and tried to explain the entire drama to Rishi after Saru left the hall because Sanjay wanted Rishi to know that Saru was the one who instigated the argument, but Rishi just grinned and asked about other friends.

Sanjay noted that Rishi had no desire to know about his strife with Saru, and he responded, "Teja and Sarad left early in the morning to see the sunrise on the beach, and they said to see you at the evening party."

Rishi: Oh, nice. Sarad shared snaps of the beautiful sunrise, which were quite captivating. Where were you yesterday? I tried to reach you, and in the morning I called you several times, but none of you even made it to Saru's birthday gathering.

Sanjay: Sorry about that. I received a recommendation to try scuba diving, which has recently gained popularity in your city. Since I had a week to spend here, I decided to do it. I felt weightless and saw incredible underwater marine creatures. When I got to the guest house at almost ten o'clock, I did not want to disturb you. Nothing beats a hot chocolate after a long day of scuba diving and a good night's sleep, and you know the rest.

Rishi: Great, get ready, and I'll wait here.

A short while later, Sanjay and Rishi prepared to leave together. As they both walked toward the cellar, they noticed that the car was already on the road, with Saru in the driver's seat and the engine running. As they both climbed inside, Saru accelerated away. Nobody said anything until they got home.

Sanjay got out of the car and waited for Saru to park it, as Rishi hurried into the house as soon as they arrived. Sanjay approached and stopped her, maintaining eye contact as he extended his hand to shake hers and requested a negotiable friendship. The question initially surprised Saru, but she quickly warmed to Sanjay's cordial approach and agreed to be friends.

Saru: Sanjay, but on one stipulation.

Sanjay: Sure, so what's that?

Saru: When the time comes, I'll ask you, Sanjay.

Sanjay: Unquestionably.

Playful Saru just couldn't resist throwing a teasing smile at Sanjay. Sanjay reciprocated with a grin. And off they went into the house. After a grand party, most of the invitees left, and the immediate relatives, in small numbers, stayed back. After the event had taken its toll on everyone's energy, it was no surprise that they all stumbled into their designated rooms for a well-deserved snooze.

Who wouldn't be exhausted after the full energy consumption event, full of drama, intrigue, excitement, and adrenaline coursing through their veins? It's enough to knock anyone out like a tranquilized rhino.

As evening fell, Rishi's friends—who had not been seen in the hotel room—finally made their grand entrance at home, and other buddies too charged out of nowhere like a pack of wolves and made their way to the pool, where they lounged around like a bunch of sloths while guzzling mixed drinks and hard drinks like it was water. Saru's girl friends, who numbered in the single digits, were unable to attend for a variety of reasons. Despite the fact that it was Saru's birthday, Rishi's friends dominated the party.

Meanwhile, the atmosphere was filled with the tantalizing aroma of finger foods as the group gorged themselves on a smorgasbord of tasty snacks. Without giving much thought to the consequences of their actions, they completely immersed themselves in the blissful party.

Contrary to what is happening in the pool, Saru is listening to calming music on her own-gifted portable digital music player, Carvaan. She lay on her pillow and rolled her hair with the index finger of her right hand as she thought back on her encounter with Sanjay earlier this morning.

A chirpy sound from her phone disturbed Saru's tranquility, and she became aware that she had also dozed off. When she opened the chat window. It was from Rishi. The message was, "Where are you? Are you still unsettled from this morning's encounter with Sanjay? Come on, Saru, there are so many handsome faces around me, including Sanjay. He he."

Saru couldn't help but grin from ear to ear as she read the text she received from Rishi; the excitement and anticipation of the upcoming evening were almost too much to bear. With each passing minute, the butterflies in her stomach seemed to proliferate, and she couldn't wait to see what the night would bring on her birthday.

After much contemplation and a few outfit changes, Saru finally settled on a simple yet elegant sleeveless gown for the party. With minimal makeup and a casual updo, she looked positively radiant, a vision of effortless beauty that would surely captivate all who laid eyes on her. Saru replied to Rishi, "Coming, I am settled and ready to meet the peacocks."

Rishi: I think you've already met a good one. Come soon, and there are a lot of options if you want more.

Saru was focused on putting herself in an elegant position as she read a text, chose not to respond to Rishi, and put the phone down. When Saru made her filmy entrance to the pool, a few men were drooling at her charm and hotness, and a few girls were fuming with jealousy; one of them sang, "Gualbhi aankhen jo teri dheki sharabhi ye dil ho gaya," but Sanjay was unfazed.

Saru blushed and grinned to herself before going to the table, getting a glass of lime water, and looking for Rishi with her two exquisite lotus-shaped scanners. When she finally found Rishi. He was surrounded by his friends on all sides, but she was able to get close to him despite the crowded, chaotic environment.

Rishi was certain that his friends would be interested in Saru because of her beauty and charm, but he managed to pull Saru away from the piercing sights and party sound effects. Rishi led her to a less crowded area where their words could be heard.

Rishi: Your entry must have raised the temperature. What are you drinking, Saru? Don't tell me that you are sipping lime water.

Saru: Ha! I heard the song too. I'm good with lime water.

Rishi: So, now, are you all set with Sanjay?

Saru: Hmmm.

Rishi: Okay, take time to rebound.

Saru: I'm not sure how long I pondered, but it was a fair amount of time, and I could have stuck at it indefinitely without taking a bite and sleeping, but after seeing your text, having risen from the bed, gotten ready, and continued to ponder, things suddenly clarified.

Rishi: I'm relieved that things have been clarified; I didn't expect you and your encounter with Sanjay to be raging, but you could have at the very least waited for me.

Saru: Agh, I kind of lost it over him, and I was eager to get to the closet of ease.

Rishi: All right, whatever happened, happened. Since today is your birthday and you have never had a margarita, do so now.

Saru winced and kept mum, opting not to take any form of alcoholic beverage.

Rishi: Okay, no trying, and please change your grimace face; I can't see it for a second.

"I can see it, and it is gorgeous," said Sanjay, holding a glass of whiskey and looking into Saru's eyes. In response to

Sanjay's honey-dipped words, Saru made a startled face, and she thought that earlier in the day, he had made accusations against her for using her own bathroom on her father's property, and now he was flattering me.

Sanjay: I know I've been bad this morning, and I've said sorry too.

Other friends called Rishi and told him they needed him. So, while Sanjay and Saru were deep in conversation, Rishi slipped away from the scene, saying, "I'll be right with you guys," and walked over to where the action was. Saru waited for Rishi to walk a little further away from them and responded.

Saru: I am the one who owes you an apology, and your apology was accepted in the morning itself.

Sanjay: Are you certain?

Saru: yes.

Sanjay: Hmm, fancy that, whiskey?

Saru: Whisky invariably, and I see you smoke as well.

Sanjay: Oh, yes, I am an occasional smoker, especially during extreme emotional states.

Saru: I have nothing to say, so do you always smoke cigarettes?

Sanjay: As I told you, I occasionally smoke, but I prefer to vape.

Saru: Well, at what age are you introduced to injurious things?

Sanjay: Certainly, at 18. What are you going to do with this information?

Saru: Well, analyzing and interpreting, ha ha.

After maintaining steady eye contact with Saru, Sanjay paused briefly before breaking into laughter in response to her laughter. He then asked, "What now?" as he continued to chuckle. There wasn't much of interest to report, as Saru retreated to her room with the anticipation of a difficult night's sleep given the extensive preparations for the upcoming day. As she settled in, she turned to her companion, addressing him with a playful grin and asking, "And what about you, Mr. Handsome?"

Sanjay: Wah! I was surprised to hear such kind things from you about me. Cheers, clinching his glass with Saru' So, I've been promoted from Mr. Moron to Mr. Handsome, which sounds pretty good. Thank you for tagging me with such kind words, and I hope to end this day on a memorable and interesting note. A good ride would be nice at this point.

Saru: This isn't too quick, and aren't you too clever to ask me for a date without actually asking me? Isn't it already too late? Rishi went back to his room; the sun was only a few hours away from greeting us with a bright morning.

Sanjay pondered the fact that Saru gave him reasons but didn't say no to my proposal. Saru was comforted by being told that She would return before sunrise and be secure in her room.

Saru: Ah, everything was preplanned, which is impressive. So, where are you taking me?

Sanjay: Not much is decided, as this is not my city. I wish you could guide me and suggest a nice place.

Saru: Well, for the opportunity, I would suggest the most favorite place of the vizagites.

Sanjay: Haha, that sounds good; let's head to the beach.

Sanjay gestures for Saru to follow. Her nonchalant response belied her inner excitement at the prospect of spending more time with Sanjay and getting to know him better. Saru couldn't help but wonder what the rest of the night had in store for them as they made their way to the car.

As they drove towards the beach, Saru expressed her love for the beaches in and around the city, especially the city beach, which she described as a peaceful place to watch the strong tides at night. Sanjay, smiling, remarked on how much Vizagites seem to love beaches.

Once they arrived, Saru insisted on sitting on the sand, and Sanjay complied. Saru knelt down and closed her eyes, taking in the sounds of the waves and the beauty of the beach in front of her.

The sand shimmered with the moonlight's luminescence. The sand itself seems to sparkle like a thousand tiny diamonds, casting a soft, glowing light that reflects off the water's surface. It was a serene moment, and Sanjay couldn't help but appreciate the simplicity of the moment they were sharing together.

Saru stated, looking at her wristwatch on her right hand, that she would prefer not to be woken up by those energetic morning walkers.

Sanjay: Funny, I, too, don't want to receive morning walkers.

Saru: Take me back home.

Sanjay: As you say, let's go.

Saru nodded her head and stood up. They both walked to the road where the car was parked, and though Saru sat beside him in the car, her eyes were on the beach.

However, no one spoke much on the way back to the house. The silence had the upper hand. Saru checked her watch as they approached the house. "Bye, see you tomorrow. Oh, sorry, I'll see you in a few hours," she says hurriedly, as she doesn't want to get caught in the eyes of anyone because her aunties have had hawk sightings. Sanjay smiled, and no words were exchanged between them.

When Sanjay opened his mouth, Saru didn't wait for his reply and dashed out of the car. Sanjay ran behind Saru after parking the car a little further away from the house to avoid the sounds made while locking the car. Saru used the cat steps on the stairs to escape the elevator's commotion.

"Hey, Saraswati, where were you until now?" In a hard voice, said Sanjay, standing behind Saru.

Saru was terrified and believed someone had seen her. She said, "No, no, I've just been out for a walk, in a stammering voice."

Isn't it too early for a walk, and did you go alone? Why are you holding your footwear in your hands?

Saru's tenseness increased, and she said, "Hmmm... shoes," looking for a reason to justify her walking comment.

Meanwhile, Sanjay let out a chuckle and said, "Relax, Saru."

Hearing Sanjay's voice, Saru turned to face him and sighed heavily.

Saru: Sanjay, you scared me, and I request that you not act this way again. I was afraid I had ruined my freedom on the first day of receiving it.

Sanjay: Freedom? Freedom from whom? Saru.

Saru: Shh… Don't shout because someone might overhear us; by this time, I think a few aunts and uncles were awake and using the restroom.

Sanjay: Hmm, okay, so tell me? Freedom? whispered.

As Sanjay drew nearer, Saru experienced an unexplainable sense of fear and anxiety. She took a few deep breaths, held Sanjay's hand, and then quietly entered her room, shut the door, and turned the knob.

When she put her ear close to the door and listened, she could hear footsteps getting louder. When she noticed someone approaching her, her cat steps became remarkably agile and light on her feet like a rat as she ran over to Sanjay, who was standing and watching everything from the single seat in the room. Saru requested that Sanjay hide somewhere.

Sanjay: Okay, relax. But why are you asking me to hide, Saru?

Saru: Someone is coming. We are both going to feed their stupid brains throughout the year if they see you and me like this. Please find a place to hide.

Sanjay: Your room is spacious and clear, with little furniture, and the curtains aren't really opaque, so there's nowhere to hide. So where do you want me to hide? or do you stash me somewhere?

Saru: Pff, please sit on the sofa with your legs folded.

Saru struggled to open the wardrobe and began searching for a thick, big quilt to cover him when she realized it had been given to the laundry. She quickly gave up on her search and hurriedly grabbed some sheets and her clothes, piled them on top of him, and then covered the rest of the sofa with them.

A knock on the door was heard, followed by another a few seconds later.

Sanjay: In the wee hours, who might be standing there on the other side of the door?

Saru: Ah, how do I know? I'm not wearing any special lenses to see what's beyond the doors. Instead, I'm using my natural lens, so wait until I open the door to see who's on the other side.

Sanjay: Oh, is that it? Order a pair.

In response to his mocking, Saru fixed him with a disapproving look and replied, "Certainly, why don't you get them for me?"

Sanjay realized it would be better if he kept his mouth shut, or else the pleasant present would turn into a war of words, so he remained silent. After a silent agreement of understanding with Sanjay, Saru dabbed her face with water, tried to have a normal look on her face, and slowly opened the door.

Rishi: Hey Saru, I have been standing here for 300 seconds. Why did you take so much time to open the door?

Saru: It's just 300 seconds, not 300 hours. Cool your jets, and It took me a while to open the door because I was in the bathroom. What do you want, Rishi?

Rishi: Oh, okay. Will you let me in or not?

Saru: Yeah, yeah, come. What's the big deal? Tell me what you want, Rishi.

Rishi: Oh yeah, I forgot to ask; the tube of toothpaste is empty, so do you have any?

Saru: What are you blabbering about? Have you gone insane?

Rishi: Or else, what? I have some important news to share with you, but you keep bugging me with your ridiculous questions. Wait, why are you tense?

Saru: Nothing is rash; everything is fine. By the way, what is the important news?

Rishi: Wait, I recognize that tense expression on your face.

Saru: No, I am perfect, Rishi.

Rishi: What are you hiding from me?

Rishi, seeing her face after passing every two to three seconds, then began searching Saru's room while giving her a small push.

Rishi: Why are these clothes piled up? Is this your room or mine? When did we exchange our rooms?

Saru: It looks like you took the phrase "monkeying around a little too literally after polishing off that bottle of whiskey!" And about these clothes, I was searching the room and the closet because I had lost my necklace.

Rishi: Well, I heard monkeys are pretty good at partying, so I figured why not give it a shot? Oh, which chain? Why are the clothes piled up on the single-seater?

Saru held Rishi's hand and tried to stop him from going towards the piled up clothes.

Rishi: I noticed the clothes were lying down, so please allow me to assist you in folding them.

Saru: Tensed. Oh, Rishi, when did you become so helpful? In any case, the wind must be to blame. Ignore it.

Rishi: The windows were closed, the fan was turned off, and you were blaming the poor wind.

Saru moved a little towards the sofa, and she stopped him again, attempting to divert his attention away from the heap of clothes. This time, Rishi completely denied her, and his eagerness grew to reach the heap of clothes.

Rishi and Saru locked eyes as a loud sneeze echoed from the corner of the room where heaps of clothes were kept, causing Saru to be yanked off of him as Rishi removed the clothing from the seat.

Saru decided not to physically restrain Rishi after imagining what would have happened in the next episode, so she let him walk across her. To Rishi's surprise, Sanjay was sitting stiffly, with his head bowed and a difficult-to-describe expression on his face.

Rishi: odd and explosive way. You! What are you doing here?

Sanjay: Hey, Rishi.

Rishi: Hey, Sanjay, what a surprise that you showed up at this time, well dressed and covered in sheets! What is happening? Does anyone feel good telling me this?

Saru: exclaimed, Rishi, there is nothing here that matches your made-up story in your brain.

Rishi: But here it is, showing and meaning something, Saru.

Saru: looking into Rishi's eyes, said, Nothing, nothing, and please stop weaving the story in your brain. I'll be able to explain, Rishi.

Rishi walked to the bed, exhaled, clutched the pillow on the bed tightly, and looked at her like a toddler eagerly waiting for his mama to tell the bedtime story.

Saru: We both went for a drive, and when we arrived here, we thought someone had seen us. I therefore asked him to barge in, and as he did, we heard your knock.

Rishi: In a sarcastic tone, Sanjay, my friend, took Saru for a drive, which, I guess, had to be along the beach.

Saru and Sanjay chose to remain silent.

Rishi: Ah, you two managed to slink out of the crowded house right in front of me. Definitely plucky. Apart from her lines, what is your take on the story? I still feel like there is something missing in Saru's lines. Why are you not saying anything?

Sanjay: Rishi, enough with the teasing! What she put in the picture was pinpoint, and I apologize for appearing at such an odd hour. You both have your cousins' time. I will take a leave.

Saru didn't want Sanjay to leave the room so quickly; she wanted him to stay a little longer, and she reasoned that asking him to stay after what had happened wouldn't look good. But Rishi noticed a hint of discomfort in her eyes and compared it to the way a young child feels when their ice cream melts in their hands just before eating. Yet he didn't stop Sanjay.

Rishi and Saru said a quick bye to Sanjay. Saru was back in her bed, and Rishi heard her say, "I should go for a ride during the day." She laughed quietly to herself.

Rishi: Twinkling his eyes, aha, without a doubt, but tell me first, how was he? Did you guys kiss?

Saru: Are you out of your mind? It was just a drive, not a date, and it was only for an hour.

Rishi: Giggling uncontrollably and mockingly, a lot can happen in an hour, Saru.

Saru: Oh, and I don't have the same privilege and experience as you do to go on dates and make a lot happen in an hour.

Rishi: It's always tough talking to and convincing you, so I should have thought twice before poking you.

Saru: laughed aloud. So from now on, think twice before poking me. What was it that you wanted to tell me, Rishi?

Rishi: Do you remember our childhood group's nerd?

Saru: You're referring to the top student in the school who always had the answers to all the questions and wore thick glasses. Doesn't he go by the name Surya?

Standing up from the bed, Rishi searched for his misplaced mobile. Despite scouring the room for several minutes, he couldn't locate it. Frustrated, he turned to Saru and requested that she give him a call. Rishi's ears perked up as he recognized the sound coming from beneath the pillow he had been clutching moments ago. He took the mobile from the spot and proceeded to unlock it. He opened the social media site and began scrolling through the collection of photos of Surya, and Saru joined him.

Saru: Aww, too handsome a face, and so many degrees after his name for his age. No more thick glasses. Cool. But why are you suddenly showing me his pictures?

Rishi: I think that the declaration of freedom is at risk of being revoked because of an undeniable meeting between you and him that your parents have scheduled.

Saru: What exactly are you saying, Rishi? I'm uncertain whether this is a prank or a joke, but I want to let you know that I am not falling for it.

Rishi: Silly, I knocked on your door in the middle of the night to deliver the most jarring news that might sabotage your recently achieved freedom.

Saru: I am sorry; I haven't realized the gravity of the situation, and I am deeply concerned about the news that you have delivered. Rishi, please clarify to me what exactly the news is and what I can do to prevent my freedom from being jeopardized.

Rishi: Uh, I am glad that you realized. To provide more detail, our parents know you'll reject the proposal and refuse to meet, so they had to invite Surya's parents and him without informing us. They had so much planned secretly, right under our noses. Lamentably, you couldn't get out of our parents' trap of Surya and his parents' web.

Saru: Oh my God, so much was expended, but how did you get to know about this? What should I do now? Rishi.

Rishi: I overheard your parents and mine discussing this after the party last night as I was walking to the room, Saru.

Saru: You still eavesdrop on our parents' private conversations; isn't that too bad? You haven't changed a little, Rishi?

Rishi: Saru, stop acting so nice. If I hadn't heard, how would you have known about Surya? Moreover, I didn't listen willingly; my ears did the job, and I have a great solution for this unforeseen problem.

Saru: Is that so, Rishi? What's that?

With a mischievous grin, Rishi teased and burst into a song, his voice carrying the funny lyrics that say, "Say yes to Surya, marry, and have children; let the pitter-patter of little feet fill our home." Ah, the perfect example of a perfect family.

Saru: What are you snickering at? If it's about marriage, you'll be married to Sindhuja before me. La, la, la, la... Ha ha..

Rishi: Haha, very funny. However, the discovery of Sanjay in your room puts a crimp in your plans.

Saru: I apologize for failing to notify you and going for a drive with him, and I have no specific interest in him.

Rishi: Okay, that's completely okay, Saru, but be careful. By the way, why are you acting like a zombie and walking around the house?

Saru couldn't shake off the weight of the situation as she contemplated her parents' idiotic set up plan to introduce her to a potential suitor. Rishi tried to comfort her, placing his hands on her shoulders and assuring her that it was simply a meeting and not a commitment to marriage. Rishi sat down on the bed beside her and promised to help her find a solution.

Despite feeling downcast, Saru was somewhat relieved to have Rishi's support and encouragement. She sighed heavily, acknowledging the complex nature of the predicament before her. Turning to Rishi, she asked what they should do next.

Rishi responded with a note of determination, insisting that while it wouldn't be easy to extricate themselves from the situation, they would do their utmost to find a way out. He explained that he needed to rest up for the exhausting day ahead and urged Saru to do the same. With a hint of teasing, he complimented her on her exotic beauty and wished her luck in winning over Surya and his menagerie.

Saru couldn't help but smile a little at Rishi's lightheartedness, but her anxiety over the situation persisted. She knew that escaping the arranged meeting with Surya would not be simple, but she took comfort in knowing that Rishi was on her side.

Compared to the previous few days, the morning was a little colder and windier. Saru is still in bed, deep asleep, cuddling her pillow, and appears to be in a dream about her wish. She was suddenly wide awake, looking like she had been sleep-drunk, and looked for her phone, which she discovered under the pillow.

Saru: What the heck? ... thirty-two missed calls, and she checked the time; it was quarter past nine o'clock. I need to get ready, or else Rishi will be here any minute to kill me.

Saru jumped out of bed like a squirrel and finished her morning routine, just like it was depicted in a cartoon about what a hurried Tom the cat would do.

After a short while, Rishi and the other people gathered to have breakfast. Rishi approached the center hall in search of Saru. It was getting late; there was no sight of Saru in the hall, so Rishi pulled out his phone and looked at it, and he perceived that there was no call from Saru or message on it, but he had missed the sight that Saru had stood in front of him.

"Turn 45 degrees, and look at the corner of the room; you see a gorgeous lady," flashed a message on Rishi's mobile.

"Thank God, Saru is here at last," he thought and grinned as he read Saru's message and replied to Saru, "Everyone here was curious and inquiring about your delay for breakfast, particularly your mom."

Rishi took a deep breath and decided that they needed to speak in person. He suggested meeting at their usual location, which is inside the house, as there were still relatives around who could easily overhear their conversation, so he changed and proposed meeting at the guest house in ten minutes.

Saru agreed but wanted to avoid being caught, and while everyone was preoccupied with their own affairs, Saru skedaddled from the crowd, arrived at the guest house, and texted Rishi, asking where he was and mentioning that she was waiting in the car.

Rishi replied to her that it would take fifteen to twenty minutes to arrive, as escaping from everyone isn't an easy task that only pros like you can do, and with a winning champion trophy as an emoji.

In the meantime, she decided to go upstairs and say hello to Sanjay. As she took the stairs to the first floor, she noticed Sanjay closing the door.

Saru: Good morning, Sanjay.

Sanjay: Hey, good morning, Saru. This is quite a surprise; I wasn't anticipating this. Fortunately, you ran into me here while coming to meet Rishi and you.

Saru: Surprise! Rishi is on the way; why don't we go inside and wait?

Sanjay said yes, and the door creaked open slowly, as if he were hesitating to reveal what lay beyond. After a brief pause, he invited Saru inside and gestured for her to take a seat. As she entered, the sight of a hallway piled high with disorganized paperwork greeted her, evoking images of covert missions from movies. Apologizing for the mess, he quickly gathered the papers, ensuring none were left behind, and stashed them away in the room.

Sanjay: hospitably, Would you like some coffee?

Saru: I would never say no to the best tonic at any time of the day, preferably with less milk.

Sanjay: Noted, and I will be here in five minutes with hot coffee.

As Saru trailed behind, positioning herself to observe Sanjay's coffee-preparing process, an unexpected incident occurred. Just as Sanjay reached for the milk in the fridge, he accidentally spilled it over Saru. A yoke part of her beautiful lavender colored gown got wet.

Sanjay was sorry and mentioned that he didn't notice that Saru was standing behind him. Saru keeps her cool and assures him that it is only a few drops and that she will take care of it. However, he appears to be shaken by the incident.

Relieved, Sanjay let out a sigh, realizing that it was only cold milk that had spilled. Saru couldn't help but grin as she turned on the faucet, beginning to wash her dress.

Sanjay, ever the considerate host, handed her a napkin to help dry off.

Saru: Thank you.

Sanjay mentioned, "You are welcome," handing Saru a cup of coffee. They both made their way to the hall and took a seat.

Saru took a sip of the coffee and commented, "Perfect, just the way I like it. Thank you, Sanjay."

Sanjay: Twice you said, Thank you. Friends don't say thank you much.

Saru: Haha, okay. I'm going to forget to use my manners from now on. So, tell me about you and your family. Where are you from?

Sanjay's cheerful expression faltered, and he became downcast upon hearing Saru's words, turning gloomy. Sensing his change in demeanor, Saru quickly apologized, understanding she had touched upon a sensitive topic. She said, "I am sorry." "I shouldn't have asked you about your family."

Sanjay: heartened her, saying, Hey, nothing to say sorry for. It's just so difficult to speak about my family. I am of the opinion that happiness is not permanent and does not last forever. Since my parents passed away in an accident a few years ago, I have been working hard and taking care of the family business. There hasn't been a day when I haven't thought about the tragedy. However, when a friend recently invited me to join him on a city tour, I decided to accept the offer. It's been a year since I took a break and spent time with friends, and I believe that this excursion would be an excellent way to break free from my monotonous daily routine.

Saru held Sanjay's hands, expressing her sympathy with a gentle squeeze. Sanjay closed his eyes and conveyed his gratitude through a formal smile, appreciating her understanding without uttering a word.

Saru noted his somber tone and understood that his responsibilities had taken precedence over indulging in the city's natural wonders. She respected his dedication but sought to provide a temporary escape from the demands of his work.

Saru, who wanted to change the topic, posed a question to Sanjay. "Why are you so focused on working with papers and files when you are in the midst of a nature-filled city?" She asked curiously.

Sanjay paused for a moment, appearing lost in thought, before responding with a somewhat vacant expression. "It's just pending office work that couldn't be postponed any longer," he explained.

Saru sensed the weight of his words and the importance he placed on his responsibilities. Nevertheless, she wanted to offer him a respite from work. In an effort to lighten the mood, she playfully commented on his choice of words earlier. "Oh, so you are always searching for the perfect words before speaking?"

With a mischievous smile, Sanjay replied, "Nah, let's just say that when a gorgeous gal enters my sights, my vocabulary goes on a scavenger hunt for the perfect words to use."

Impressed by his wit, Saru expressed her admiration. "Smart and sly, too," she remarked. She then suggested they go shopping together, hoping to provide Sanjay with a chance to relax and clear his mind. Sanjay's face lit up, reflecting his eagerness to join her.

Sanjay: Just what I was going to ask you. And of course, I would love to join.

Rishi: Hey guys! Good morning, Sanjay.

Sanjay: Hey, Rishi, we're waiting for you to join us.

Rishi: Saru and Sanjay, excuse me. It was difficult to get away from everyone, especially with my mother and aunt present. I have to drive back home as I don't have much free time.

Sanjay: Hey Rishi, What's the hurry? You just came, right?

Rishi: Sanjay, why don't you come home with us?

Sanjay: Yes, I was coming to see you guys, and Saru showed up.

Rishi: Oh, we've talked about meeting at the guest house.

Sanjay: You sound a little off, Rishi. Is there anything I can do to help?

Without uttering a single word, Rishi enveloped Sanjay in a tight bear hug, his elation evident in his voice as he proclaimed, "You are a lifesaver, Sanjay! Saru's problem is now solved."

Confusion clouded Sanjay's face as he sought an explanation, asking Rishi, "What are you talking about?" Rishi swiftly motioned for him to be silent, indicating the need for discretion.

Saru interjected with concern, cautioning Rishi, "No, Rishi! Don't drag Sanjay into this." Sanjay, perplexed by the unfolding situation, sought clarification, asking, "What is going on, guys?"

Taking charge, Rishi unveiled his plan, sharing with Sanjay, "You will be playing the role of Saru's boyfriend." Sanjay's disbelief was evident as he exclaimed, "Wait, what? You want me to pretend to be Saru's boyfriend? Can someone please explain this to me?"

Sensing the need for privacy, Saru guided Rishi to a secluded corner of the room. Their voices lowered as they engaged in a discussion.

Saru voiced her concerns, requesting clarification from Rishi, "Why rush into involving Sanjay? Is it really necessary? "What's your plan?"

Rishi attempted to assuage her worries, saying, "Just relax, Saru. As I mentioned earlier, Surya's family, whom our parents invited, has already arrived, and Surya himself will be here in an hour.

We can ask Sanjay to act as your boyfriend until my engagement ceremony.

Saru remained skeptical, pressing Rishi further, "But even if they have reached the airport, why complicate things by involving Sanjay?"

Rishi: If we can persuade Surya that Sanjay is your boyfriend, he'll drop the marriage proposal on his own, Saru.

Saru: What you just said is not right; everything appears chaotic and incorrect to me. I'll rush to the airport and explain it to him before he gets there.

Rishi: What do you think, Saru? Will he respect, accept, and agree with your decision? Remember, during school time, he never listened to anyone; he did what came to his mind.

Saru: Yes, Rishi, he was adamant, but what if he has changed?

Rishi: He wouldn't have changed; I am certain of that. Remember your last meeting with him, when he told you he liked you, but what did you do?

Saru: Ha, I was just fifteen, and you hope that he will remember the incident?

Rishi: Due to your action of sharing the news with the entire class and it subsequently spreading throughout the entire campus, our classmates, seniors and even juniors, teased him so severely that he ended up giving complaints against you to the school head.

Saru: Yeah, I was grief-stricken considering the principal's words; it was a disastrous chapter in the school book, Rishi. He once had a crush on me, but it was clearly only puppy love, which was ages ago.

Rishi: But, Saru, what my instincts strongly suggest is that going to the airport, meeting him, and convincing him doesn't give us the output we wanted.

Saru: Then what do we do now, Rishi?

Rishi: As I said earlier, let's get help from Sanjay.

Saru: Hmm. Okay, but I'm not going to ask him because, to be completely honest, my worries are greater.

Rishi: You just nod your head and say "yes." I will convince him, Saru.

Upon emerging from the room, Rishi and Saru were surprised to find Sanjay waiting just outside, having overheard their conversation. Sanjay greeted them, apologizing for eavesdropping but expressing his enthusiasm about the idea of pretending to be Saru's boyfriend.

Confusion washed over Rishi and Saru as they both exclaimed, "What?" They couldn't comprehend why Sanjay was so willing to take on this role.

Sanjay clarified his intentions, stating his willingness to act as Saru's temporary boyfriend.

Rishi and Saru were taken aback, grappling with the sudden acceptance and agreement from Sanjay, fully aware that such an arrangement could potentially lead to complications in the future. In unison, Rishi and Saru expressed their gratitude, saying, "Thank you, Sanjay." Sanjay responded with a beaming smile, "Anything for Rishi, and of course for you too, Saru."

Curious about the next steps, Sanjay inquired about the plan.

Caught off guard by the unexpected turn of events, Rishi found himself ill-prepared to handle the situation at hand. He openly admitted that he hadn't anticipated this scenario, and while he was grateful for Sanjay's willingness and suggestion, he excused himself and headed home urgently. With a sense of urgency, Rishi took his leave, leaving the remaining individuals in a state of uncertainty, unsure of what steps to take next and how the situation would unfold.

Sanjay: Hey, Saru, I'm referring to the fact that I'm willing to serve as a stand-in boyfriend for you for the time being.

Saru: Is the plan still in effect?

Sanjay: Saru, haven't you heard his words? He hasn't made a decision, and I am not sure whether he will consider my offer. So I'm not sure.

Saru: Not sure? What happened after you said you wanted to go shopping a few minutes ago? Wait, it seems that you're very keen on taking on the role of my boyfriend, which highlights your strong interest in this role.

Sanjay: I guess you just unlocked my romantic circuits.

Saru: Whattt?

Sanjay: Saru, I was pulling your legs; I was just distracted and missed the connectivity. I don't understand anything here; Rishi is the one who wanted my help, which he denied when I was ready to help, and if you're still planning to shop, then yes, before we conquer the shopping world, let's fuel up with some grub.

Saru: Okay, but there's nothing to worry about considering Rishi's words; some other idea might have knocked him out. About breakfast, mine was filling, and I am full. So, I will satisfy my eyes but not my stomach, and what do you like to eat for breakfast?

Sanjay: Saru, Cool, I won't coerce you to consume food. When it comes to choices, I am not picky or particular, and anything that fills my stomach is fine with me.

Saru: Haha… so. Given that it's a little too early for lunch and too late for breakfast, why don't you have brunch?

Sanjay: That sounds good, Saru.

Sanjay started the vehicle to go to a restaurant for brunch. Saru's mobile phone vibrated; it was Rishi.

Saru: Hello, Rishi, tell me.

Rishi: I have been sending you messages; why are you not replying to any of them?

Saru: Oh, my mobile is in silent mode. What's the rush? Sanjay went to get the vehicle; we both plan to go for brunch; later, we'll go shopping; and we'll see you in the evening.

Rishi: Right away, cancel all of your plans and return to the residence. Surya and his parents were on their way home and could arrive at any time. Your parents are asking about you and repeating the same question twenty times per second like a woodpecker pecking at the wood, and I just escaped from their sight before they foraged me like a woodpecker for insect prey, and I request that you be here.

Saru: Uff... I'm not coming, and I'm going to brunch with my temporary boyfriend, hehe. You manage or manipulate, but I will not return before evening.

Rishi: This is insane. How could I manage your parents and mine? Don't leave me to them. Saru, once you give over the mobile to Sanjay,

Saru: why? Don't ruin my time with him; this is the first time I've had the opportunity to go out with someone other than you.

Rishi: Saru, I completely comprehend, but this moment is not the right one. Consider this: Why should you welcome more problems?

Saru: solemnly, all right, don't lecture me now. I'll come right away.

Rishi: Perk up. Don't bring Sanjay along with you.

Saru: Why? But why? When did you become a chameleon? Finally, even though the opportunity to have a boyfriend is only valid for a few days, I would bring him and proudly declare him to be my boyfriend, so I'll be relieved of tension from Surya and the gang of aunts, and I'll be at least content and secure until your wedding, but you didn't make it last for even a few minutes.

Hmm,..

Saru: Rishi, What exactly are you envisioning?

Rishi: You will remember that I was thinking about this and was still wondering why Sanjay had accepted our request for assistance and why he had done so quickly.

I simply gave up the idea of bringing him into this particular scene and concentrated on a part of the situation that had been puzzling me from the beginning.

Saru: Don't put it that way; it seemed like an admirable opportunity to know about him up close and personal. I believe I should take advantage of the opportunity to be his girlfriend.

Rishi: Saru, what is this you are talking about? It seems like you have taken my words seriously. He is certainly handsome and has a good heart, but why does everything have to be rushed?

Saru: Oh, did you say this? Rushed ? In a nutshell, I just want to go for brunch and have fun, and on that note, he is handsome and a friend of yours. Rishi, I see Sanjay coming up to me.

Rishi: That's my girl! But remember, if you get caught in the eyes of family, brace yourself for an interrogation, and it's like a barrage of questions and doubts launched from a confetti cannon. See you.

Saru: Yes, I am aware and I am dropping the phone call. I'll be home.

Sanjay: Hey, Saru. Ready for the long day?

Saru: uncomfortably, with a sad tone, Hey, Sanju.

Sanjay: Hey, hey, all good? You seemed to be low. You were doing well just a few minutes ago.

Saru: Hmm, Rishi called and asked me to return home swiftly. So, I am sorry. Sometime later, we will plan a brunch.

Sanjay: Oh, that's it. No problem. Shall I drop you off at home?

Saru: That would be very nice of you, and we will plan an outing sometime in the coming days.

Sanjay dropped Saru off at her house, and when she invited him to come in, he declined, saying he was hungry and would go get some food.

Saru: Okay, Sanjay, See you later, and take care.

Sanjay left the place, and Saru walked straight into her room, escaping from the people in her path smartly. She saw her mom and Rishi at the entrance of her room.

Mrs. Sharmila: Hey, Rishi, I'm worried about your cousin Saraswati because of the instantaneous planned meeting with Surya's family, which your uncle promptly extended an invitation to.

Rishi: Oh, Aunty, they've already reached so fast.

Mrs.Sharmila: What ? Why did you use such an expression as if you knew about this arrangement? How do you know about this meeting? Rishi, I am talking to you, and I expect a proper answer from you.

Rishi: Ha, Aunty. Give me a break; don't be serious. I could see deep furrows on your lower forehead.

Mrs. Sharmila: Well, well, my dear nephew, it seems that my thoughts are to blame for my brow-furrowing. My forehead will be wrinkle-free in the face of your delightful antics if you tell me exactly how you know.

Rishi: I meant, Oh, they came, and why are you so worried? Shall I reveal a well kept secret to you?

Mrs. Sharmila: What did she do again? I know, you guys' imagination has no boundaries. So, tell me? Do you guys have any travel plans?

Rishi: Nah, relax, Aunty. You seem so young for your age. One of my friends recently remarked, Does Saru have an older sister?

Mrs. Sharmila: Blushing, Rishi, stop icing.

Rishi: Promise me one thing, Aunty. Don't get upset over insignificant things; you don't look good with wrinkles. Let the worries dissipate like morning mist, and let our hearts be filled with the lightness of laughter.

Mrs. Sharmila: Haha, I appreciate that you and Saru have turned into remarkable individuals with wisdom gained through the passage of time. Rishi, now tell me how you know about this meeting. Is Saru aware of it? So, not showing up right now and not returning calls were part of the plan?

Rishi replied with a silvery laugh, no.

Mrs. Sharmila: Saru is not answering my calls; I don't know how to contact her, but I want her to be here in ten minutes.

Rishi, feeling uneasy, maintained a solemn silence and reached for his phone to call Saru. Meanwhile, as Saru noticed her mother leaving the place, she hurriedly answered Rishi's call and urged him to join her inside.

As Rishi stepped into the room, Saru eagerly confronted him about her current position. She inquired about her mother's words and sought Rishi's advice on whether she should proceed with a fashion show for Surya and his parents or engage in a confrontation with her mom regarding the lack of communication about the arrangements.

Curious about her mother's sentiments, Saru questioned Rishi about their conversation. Rishi shared that her mother seemed deeply concerned during their interaction, revealing a side of her he had never witnessed before. But Saru, confidently and with a playful wink, teasingly insinuated that Rishi must have done something or said something to capture her mother's attention.

Rishi: Yay, now that I've done it, you must have seen her. You should have returned her call at least once; it wouldn't have caused her to flinch.

Saru: Hmm, I came back as quick as a flash. What now?

Rishi: The audience was expecting you, so get ready, and I am leaving.

With the door wide open, Mrs. Sharmila entered the room, carrying a beautiful carved vintage wooden box. Saru greeted her mother, explaining that she hadn't responded to the phone call as her phone was on silent mode. Instead, she opted to meet her in person when she realized she was near her home. Curiosity sparked within Saru as she wondered about the contents of the intriguing wooden box her mother gave her.

Saru responded to Mrs. Sharmila's inquiry by manipulating and revealing that she had gone out with a friend to a nearby cafe just a few blocks away from their home. She pondered that the meeting with Rishi beyond the doorstep and the chat with Sanjay held importance; if she explains her concerns to her mother with pinpoint details, She will end up with a flux of explanations for her mom, and Saru assured her mother that nothing would be done against her wishes.

With a knowing grin, Saru recognized that engaging in a logical discussion with her mother would lead to a chain of illogical arguments. In an effort to maintain peace and avoid unnecessary debates, she chose to remain silent, appreciating the harmonious surroundings that enveloped them.

Mrs. Sharmila and Rishi walked to the door with relaxed expressions when they realized Saru had arrived on time, even though their motives were different. Mrs. Sharmila paused, turned, and said, "Don't forget to put on some jewelry."

Saru sighed.

After a few minutes, having received the message from Saru, Rishi went back to the room and was shocked and amazed to see Saru wearing a cherry red chikankari kurta with sparsely attached mirrors and a pair of plain, straight-leg white pants with matching jumkas with hanging white pearls and minimal makeup.

When Saru turned her head to the side and saw Rishi in the mirror, she got to her feet and asked,

"How do I look?"

Rishi kept staring at her despite not understanding a word she said because of how stunning she was.

Saru: Rishi, Rishi, how do I look? How many times should I ask you?

Rishi: Ya, you do look lovely, Saru. I still see some costume jewelry left on the table.

Saru: I had enough on me, so how much is some?

Rishi: Hmm. You were born with natural jewelry—your kind heart and warm smile. So, in reality, you don't need much.

Saru: blushed, But I need you by my side, Rishi.

Rishi: Oh, I'll be there. Pay attention and maintain your composure.

Saru: Now what? Saying and mockingly laughing, will you teach me how to walk and talk in front of them?

Rishi: How can I teach you to walk and talk? Haha, does someone teach peacocks to dance? Does someone teach monkeys to leap from tree to tree? Does someone teach dolphins to be social and friendly? What I mean to say is that you were born talented and beautiful.

Saru: Oh my god, stop watching the Discovery Channel right away; you watch too many animal programs.

Rishi: Bla bla... and don't suffocate the poor soul, Surya, with your beauty and questionnaire.

Saru: Haha. Who knows, he might suffocate me in return, but not with his charm.

On their way to the main hall of the house, Rishi and Saru nagged at one another. When they arrived, they saw Surya sitting by himself in the chair that had been separated from the rest of the big sofa.

To their shock, only the main male judge was in the show and was sipping coffee like the show had already been a success before it even started, and Rishi and Saru tightened muscles around their eyes and searched for the other judges and audience.

Rishi whispered, “All the best to Saru’s ears.”

Saru: Don’t leave me with him, you idiot; he is a complete stranger to me.

Rishi: I presumed you would say this. If you ask me, rather than performing the talents and answering the viva in front of a large audience, this is preferable because there is only one audience member.

Saru: Yah, a little concession.

As Surya and Rishi exchanged polite small talk, Rishi said, I’ll see you soon, to Surya and left.

Surya, who looked handsome with defined facial features and a symmetrical face with clear skin, had a crafty look. He took off his spectacles, polished them with a soft cloth taken from the trouser’s pocket, put them on again, and wished, “Hi to Saraswati.”

Saru greeted Surya with a warm smile. Surya, in turn, responded and acknowledged the pleasure of meeting Saru.

His eyes couldn't help but linger on her, and he complimented her, "Saru, you are truly captivating, and your beauty shines."

Saru: I know, Surya. It's no wonder you find me beautiful. I radiate irresistible charm. Is it enough to marry me?

Surya: No manners? And perhaps not. Despite the fact that you were exactly the same as I imagined you to be, I still wanted to meet you and have an open heart chat with you today.

Saru: Mockingly, Oh, what exactly have I done to merit such a wonderful opportunity?

Surya: No matter what, I am interested in you and eager to know everything there is to know about you before I take a step towards marriage, but before that, I have some obligations.

Saru: Oh, marriage, ah? Obligations?

Surya: I don't much like the sound of this.

Saru: Sarcastically, Uff. Then am I allowed to make this sound?

Surya: You are more haughty than I thought. Isnt ?

Saru: You are much more adamant than I had imagined, isn't that right?

Surya let out a sinisterly toned laugh, and the way he looked at her in that moment was unsettling, filling her with a deep sense of uneasiness and making her anxious to stay for another second. He continuously troubled her by asking incoherent questions, which added to her growing anxiety.

Saru felt overwhelmed by the constant barrage of questions and attention from Surya; she longed for someone to come and interrupt and liberate her from his torment. It seemed impossible to escape Surya's grisly and disgusting looks. To avoid Surya's gaze, she walked closer to the window, slowly pushed it open, hiding her hands under the curtain, and acted as if she were listening to him. She picked up the ball from the bowl near the window and threw it out the window.

In two minutes, Max and Leo arrived at the uninteresting show, with Leo wagging his tail and holding the ball between his harrumphing teeth.

As soon as her canine friends arrive, Saru notices them and beams a contented smile.

Surya struggled to hide his uncomfortable and irritated expression from Saru when the dogs showed up. However, he was unable to conceal his annoyance and asked, "Could you send the dogs away?"

Before Saru could respond, Max growled at Surya and turned his head away, and Leo didn't bother bothering him. Saru knelt on the floor and rubbed her palms against Max's and Leo's bodies, saying, "They just came and wanted to play ball with them."

Surya: Oh, then you guys can play out of my sight.

Saru: inwardly chuckled, We've had our fill of talking, right? And this is my house.

Surya: Yes, this is your house. Are you consistently rude to guests who are invited to your home? Of course, we can meet later. Over the course of a week, I will be in this city.

Saru: Hesitantly. Nah, I am good with good and bad with bad. It is especially dependent on the behavior of the guests, and you are staying here for a duration of seven days?

Surya: Yea. My only goal is to get to know you better. If you'd like, I'd like to meet and hang out with you for a full week. If it's ok with you, let's get together at some point for any meal of the day.

Saru attempted to politely decline his invitation, but she was unsuccessful. She then considered what she might have to say in response to his response and chose to remain silent.

Taking Saru's initial silence as a positive indication, the assumption was made that she would be available the next day to meet him. However, feeling uneasy about the situation she was in, Saru eventually mustered the courage to address the matter, stating, "I appreciate the invitation, but I must decline this time."

After listening to Saru's words, Surya moved closer to her to speak out, but Max barked just as he was about to start speaking, and Saru's parents and Surya's parents all walked into the hall.

By taking deep breaths and letting go of the tension in her body as she watched everyone move towards them, she was able to relax her tense muscles. She then made eye contact with everyone while grinning.

Mrs. Sharmila was relieved that Saru and Surya had finally met, had a quick chat, and that she had formally introduced the two families. For a split second, she thought Surya was not the right person for her daughter. But what was going on there quickly overshadowed that.

After a while, Surya and his family headed for the hotel. Saru's parents returned to their busy routine, and Rishi's parents joined them.

Saru strolled aimlessly to her room and asked Sita to bring her a persimmon smoothie with fruit slices and chia seeds. As she used the restroom and changed into comfortable clothes, Sita placed the shake on the table, and Saru gulped in a shot and messaged Rishi that she would meet and share the details of the disastrous meeting in the evening. A powerful nap is much needed to recover from Surya's stupid actions, and she passes out.

It was fifteen minutes before six in the evening, and all relatives had emptied. The house is peaceful as well. When Saru got up from the bed and opened her eyes, she noticed Rishi waiting for her to awaken.

Hey Rishi.

Hey Saru, How are you feeling now?

Saru: I am feeling more energetic and focused and less stressed and irritable.

Rishi: So you got some mental benefit from your sleep, which is fine and lucky. So, how was your encounter with Surya? He has brought you a lovely bouquet. Did he invite you for lunch or dinner?

Saru: Uhh, the bouquet is elegant with attractive and spectacular blooms. About him, I found it extraordinarily difficult to believe that, to have reached this status and fame, he must be an ass. Surya did not appear to me to possess a single lovable quality. He looked like a villain out of a commercial film where both the hero and villain have tough roles to justify.

Rishi: Cool off, Saru. The audience will be waiting and expecting you to take the second step after the first one was successful, especially your mom, so what did you decide?

Saru: How could you say it was successful?

Rishi: Of course, Saru, you might or might not like him, but parents claim the initial step was successful because the meeting was completed.

Saru: The first meeting or step was bitter, and it's like I can't even live in the same city if he lives there.

Rishi: chuckled and replied, Of course, and I wasn't a bit surprised, but how do you convince or inform your parents?

Saru: Yeah. I have to think about it, and I am certain that I will exercise my right to freedom of expression to express my feelings and opinions, and they will respect my choice, even though I am aware that they have their own reservations and worries about my marriage partner.

Just then, Rishi and Saru heard a knock on the door, which interrupted their conversation. Rishi expressed, "Who might be there now? Are you expecting anyone?" to which Saru replied in the negative. Curiosity piqued, Rishi volunteered to answer the door, while Saru hesitated and was unsure about who could be on the other side.

Mrs.Sharmila: Hi Rishi, I knew you both would be here, as you are her happy pill, and you will make my visit easy.

Rishi smiled and remained silent, allowing the conversation to unfold.

Mrs.Sharmila: Where is your partner in crime?

Saru: Hi, Mom.

Mrs.Sharmila: Hi Saru, Why didn't you join us for lunch? Why did you skip lunch, dear?

Saru: I didn't feel the need to eat lunch because my breakfast had left me feeling satisfied.

Mrs.Sharmila: Aw, I haven't seen you since the morning, and you weren't in the dining room for breakfast.

Saru: Mom, as I already mentioned, went down to meet a friend.

Mrs.Sharmila: Oh, for breakfast? Without Rishi?

Cough…

Mrs.Sharmila gave Rishi a sharp, skeptical look as he coughed purposefully, making a rough, raspy sound. Saru gave him a black look for coughing on purpose and turned to face her mother, explaining that she didn't eat lunch today because she wasn't particularly hungry and that she had a fruit shake.

Saru: Ask Sita if you don't believe me.

Mrs.Sharmila: One more lie?

Saru: Mom, it's just so funny! I can't believe you think I am lying about skipping lunch. Believe me.

Mrs.Sharmila: What is so funny that you laughed out loud?

Saru: “Nothing, mom.”

Mrs.Sharmila: “Even if it’s just for fun, you must stop lying because it can hurt you or those around you by shattering relationships that you already have or will develop in the future. I know my lengthy explanations have annoyed and frustrated you, but what should you do, sweet little angel? If not me, who will advise you, Saru?”

Saru: Look at me, Mom; I’m cool and cheerful. Despite my assurances to the contrary, I have to admit that I appreciate your willingness and patience to explain. But, Mom, I have to admit that I’m feeling a little overrun and overwhelmed right now.

Mrs.Sharmila: Okay, Saru, I respect your feelings and opinions, and I do understand them. Do you feel like eating right now?

Saru wrapped her mother in a tight bear momma hug, assuring that “she is fine and not hungry.” Her embrace conveyed a sense of warmth and affection, comforting both of them in that moment.

Rishi, observing the touching scene, couldn’t contain his excitement. He exclaimed, “Wow, did you see that, Saru? Aunty doesn’t have any more wrinkles!” He eagerly joined in the embrace, enveloping them in his arms.

Mrs.Sharmila chuckled at Rishi’s lighthearted comment. Despite the late hour, she suggested, “You two should at least join us for dinner.”

Rishi immediately responded, “Count us in, and don’t forget to include my preferences of some delicious aloo parathas with large amounts of ghee on both sides, and for the dessert, we must have carrot halwa.” Saru added, “Yes, with a layer of milk khoa, topped with finely chopped almonds and pumpkin seeds. But no raisins, please, as in the detail of Rishi’s preference.”

Rishi beamed at the thought of such a delightful meal. “Blissful,” he remarked, his anticipation evident in his voice. Mrs.Sharmila bid them farewell, saying, "See you both later," as she gratefully exited the room, leaving behind a sense of warmth and excitement for the upcoming dinner.

Rishi and Saru lay side by side on the bed, gazing up at the roof. Rishi’s question raised Saru’s curiosity, causing her brow to furrow slightly. Saru comforted Rishi by saying that her mom probably hadn’t heard their conversation about Surya, emphasizing her respect for her privacy. They both agreed that it was important to be mindful of their volume and to share personal matters at their own pace.

Saru: Rishi, My mind was spinning endlessly with the same questions, much like planets around the sun.

Rishi: What now?

Saru: I’ll tell Mom about Surya when she inquires. But now that I can’t afford to waste time rambling on about topics I don’t care about, let’s waste the time on things like bowling, dining, and other frivolous activities.

Rishi: Yeah, that sounds like a perfect plan for me. Compared to lying on the bed and staring at the roof, this sounds preferable. Are you interested in inviting someone?

Saru: Shyly, I don't mind if you invite Sanjay.

Rishi: Aww, look at you; you've never been such a shrinking violet.

Saru: You've been having a lot of fun lampooning me, considering recent episodes.

Rishi: Hehe…

Saru: So, is it yes or no?

Rishi: Is there any ambiguity? It's a yes from my side.

Hearing this, Saru decided to make a call to Sanjay; there was no answer, so she called once again, hoping for a positive outcome. To her surprise, he answered the phone on the second attempt. Saru greeted him warmly and mentioned that she had not received any messages or calls from him.

Sanjay replied, explaining that he was occupied and living alone due to his preferences and choices for independence. Saru struggles to hear his response clearly over the surrounding noise, but he dismisses it and asks if he would be interested in joining her and Rishi for a game, specifically bowling. However, Sanjay regretfully declined the invitation, mentioning that he was currently busy. Saru accepted his response graciously, said "okay," and ended the call.

Rishi: Hey, Saru, I know the reason behind your gloomy face is because he denied your invitation; is that correct?

Saru: Yeah, but how did you feel so certain about his response? And his sense of humor was convincingly quirky.

Rishi: Separation anxiety.

Saru: What is that now? And what to do with me?

Rishi: Sanjay's anxiety about being separated from loved ones grew after he lost his parents in a traumatic event. This fear grew as he experienced the people he loved leaving him alone, and it continued until he sought help from a mental health professional.

Saru: Okay, I'm sorry about him, but now he must be doing fine, right?

Rishi: Oh, yes, but when we asked him to assist us in playing the role of your temporary boyfriend, he spontaneously said "yes," which concerned me a little and caused me to think about it, and it had been years since we hadn't spoken for a few months before he made contact. What if he takes these passing events seriously?

Saru: Hmm. I see. It's understandable that you're concerned about the situation. Since he agreed to play the role of my temporary boyfriend and you haven't spoken for a few months prior to this, it's natural to wonder if he might develop genuine feelings for you under these circumstances.

Rishi: Despite the fact that I am fully aware of how you must feel, I won't risk getting you into any trouble. He's doing well now, but he might have avoided our invitation on purpose. But even though I only gave you information about his past, I'll still invite him if I still believe that his presence will make you happy.

Saru: After a brief moment of reflection, After today's morning encounter with him, I feel something off about him, or else I may be looking more deeply into it. The puzzle pieces appeared to have fallen into place, and my concerns about Sanjay were no longer figments of my imagination. Knowing that my intuition had been correct was a relief. Now that I am able to follow and connect with everything, I was a little upset when you said no. Sanjay seemed to have good and humorous instincts aside from our initial encounter, but something was wrong, and you did a good job of letting me know a little bit about him through his past.

Rishi: Ha, well, it's also a relief for me to share with you, right? We'll then give Sanjay some time to respond to us on his own terms. Then shall we go to the games now?

Saru: Yes, I must have my hair cut before that because your engagement is in a few days, and I want my hair to bounce like in the commercials.

No

Yes

But no,

But why?

Rishi: You'll say haircut, but you'll end up getting everything else done as well.

Saru: Hehe, you hit the nail on the head.

Rishi: What about games?

Saru: Let's divide up the time we have left in the evening between getting haircuts and playing games.

Rishi: Haha, I know you. Allow me to give you a clear picture of the upcoming program. I am aware that there won't be any games tonight because, if we go to the hair studio, we won't be leaving for four to five hours.

Saru: laughed jovially; you get me so well, Rishi.

Rishi: Huh, okay. But to get to the hair salon, we need to change our course right now. Did you see the congestion? The traffic was snarled up from all directions; clearly, it will take around twenty minutes. We were on the verge of arriving at the location, and I was excited that we would only be spending the rest of the day playing games.

Saru: After much convincing, you finally agreed to come to the studio, but as soon as I sealed the deal, you started looking for excuses not to go, citing traffic as one of them.

Rishi: Agh, okay. What are you searching for in the car? Did you lose anything?

Saru: Hmm, the lamp.

Rishi: What lamp?

Saru: If I find the lamp quickly, immediately after rubbing it, I might be able to get the genie's help, who will transport us to the studio without explanation because he obeys my commands.

Rishi gave her a look, snickered, and snickered again, causing Saru to burst into boisterous laughter, and she expressed, "Exuberance is exactly what we need right now."

With their cheerful spirits intact, when they arrived at the hair salon in the bustling center of the city, Rishi pushed the fanciful, ornate glass door open. The waiting area was filled with five to six people, all eagerly seeking makeovers, and impatience could be seen on their faces because of the long waiting hours.

Rishi: Did you just see the crowd, Saaaaaru? So there will be no games tonight.

Saru: Hey, Rishi. Fortunately, we arrived on time, and since I had made an appointment when we started at home, we would have been the next.

Rishi: You carried out your plan exactly, so does that imply that playing games was not even on the list?

Hehe…

Rishi: One question: why did you say "we"? Did we come here specifically for me? Saru, would you please tell me? Why did you bring me here?

The receptionist: Hello Sir, are you Mr. Rishi?

Yes.

The receptionist: You can proceed with your requested service now; please walk towards your right and continue until you reach the third room. This room has been designated for your appointment.

Rishi: Ignore the receptionist's words; hold a minute, Saru. I was truly surprised by this out of the blue salon appointment. But, you see, I have to protect my precious, irresistibly handsome face, and I can't risk anything that could damage my charm. I'll have to pass on this one; let's keep the face intact, shall we?

Saru: Oh, come on, now, don't be a spoiled brat! Your handsome face deserves more pampering and sprucing up. Let the salon service work its magic. It's like giving your charm a turbo boost!

Saru playfully nudged Rishi into the chamber, like a teacher reluctantly leading a crying child into the classroom.

"Hello, sir," greeted one of the salon staff. Rishi responded with a simple "Hi," still unsure and apprehensive about the upcoming makeover. As the staff member asked if he was ready for the transformation, Rishi hesitated, pleading, "Hey, please, I can't just sit here and let him touch me."

Saru, determined to see things through, firmly declared, "You are getting it done today." Reluctantly, Rishi accepted and realized he couldn't deny the inevitable. He knew that resisting further would only add to his embarrassment, especially as he noticed the staff already exchanging amused giggles.

Two hours later, Rishi emerged from the room with a completely new avatar, revealing the results of the transformation of the new avatar. He approached the waiting area and greeted Saru.

"Excuse me, sir." "Do I know you?" "Oh, Rishi, it's you!" she exclaimed, her eyes widening in surprise. As she realized his new appearance, a smile tugged at the corners of his lips. You look absolutely fantastic, she continued, her words filling him with a sense of accomplishment. Rishi's happiness gushed out like water from a broken pipe.

Saru: What happened to your mustache?

Rishi: I've shaved off my mustache and sacrificed in the pursuit of a happy transformation because you asked to see me without it.

Saru: What? You got rid of the mustache. You had developed an attachment to your mustache, and it had become a part of your pride and identity. How did you do it? You loved the little thing on your face.

Rishi: Yes, it has been my constant companion since puberty. A recognizable presence that represented my transition into adulthood. Bittersweet was letting it go.

Saru: Hehe, well, this extra makeover didn't seem bad. Change is always uplifting, and this is much better. But what bothers me is that you'll rue it for the next few days when you look in the mirror with no mustache.

Rishi: uff… Yes, I have to admit that missing my beloved mustache leaves a void that will linger in my mind for days.

Saru: Okay, okay. We've had enough drama for the day; now that we have some free time, how about we go bowling, Rishi?

Rishi: No, I am not comfortable and don't feel confident going in public with no mustache on my face; it's like the most valuable part of me is missing.

Saru: Rishi, Haven't I told you that you look great over and over again? Moreover, it is only hair and will grow back in a few days. In case you still don't get it, I will plan for some customized ones.

Saru clasped Rishi's arm, and he held her hand while embracing her. They exchanged smiles and affectionate gestures, and they hugged. Rishi cherished the embrace, wanting it to last longer, and he gave her a look that could have passed for affection.

Saru: Hey, after my brief trip, I waited for you to speak because your actions and behavior had made me reflect deeply. However, last night, despite my repeated questions, you chose to ignore me. Are things going well for you? You can share your burdens with me, just as I share my problems with you.

Rishi: face had lost its kind look. Hmm, aren't we getting late? Remember, Aunt asked us to join them for dinner, so we should be going now.

Saru: Oh, as I recall, her instructions and mandates are nothing new to us, and we'll deal with them as usual. The catch is that you will soon be engaged, which will be followed by a wedding. Where will we find time for outings and other things? I was just gone for a few weeks, and when I returned, you shocked me with your love news.

Rishi: Between us, Saru, nothing will alter.

Saru: See, even now, you haven't slipped a word from your mouth to me about your love affair with Sindhu. Despite the fact that I made a wordless protest after knowing the news for a day or two,

Rishi: What's the hurry? will tell you every single thing.

Saru: I think not. I've heard and seen many people say similar things as you, but weddings change relationships and dynamics; people change and their priorities shift, and you have already turned even before getting engaged. Ah, I won't be fitting into your plans any more.

Rishi: Nah, I just remembered; we need to make a list of friends for engagement and give it to Sharmila's aunty tonight.

Saru: Please, Rishi, allow me to vent, and from now on, my concerns will be less outweighed in the future, and yours were no exception in the name of marriage.

Rishi: Oh, you're certain about what you just said about everyone else, but not about us. The bond we share is unbreakable, and it is too strong to be broken by anyone or anything, and we will always be there for each other. It's us, and we stand out from the crowd. Please now insert a cheerful smile and delete the dejected look.

Saru: Then tell me; as you may know, dad often says, "Don't stretch it until it breaks." This is the last time I'm asking you to speak, so please say everything you have to say.

Rishi: Saru, I'll take you home. I don't have time for all this, so let's go.

Saru's thoughts and fears were more confirmed by Rishi's irrelevant response, and she decided to wait a few days for him to open up rather than pushing the issue further. They didn't talk much while driving; when Rishi's phone rang, he saw the number on the screen but ignored it and kept driving. It rang again, which he ignored and continued to drive. It rang again and again, which he ignored.

Saru: Attend the call; someone might be in a situation where they need your help.

Rishi carelessly dismissed the issue, saying that it was not important; just ignore it, and these incoming calls must be random or might be spasm calls. He then took the phone, turned it off, and placed it on the console.

Saru remained silent. She swiveled to the side opposite him, watching the nearby buildings, people, and trees with a sunken face, concerned about his new behavior. As they disembarked the vehicle, they went their separate ways to their homes. Saru turned and felt bad as Rishi walked inside without looking back, and she wondered where they were usually expected to hustle and contend for what they desired from one another. However, this time, things went awry, which only made Saru pout more.

In a while, Mr. Mukesh, called Rishi, was informed to come home over dinner as everyone else had gathered there with the exception of Saru and Rishi. Rishi, after his discord with Saru, opted to forgo his dinner because he was upset about what had happened between them. However, after receiving a call from his uncle, he changed his mind and considered having dinner with the family.

Rishi walked to the dining room and sat at the table, constantly keeping an eye out for Saru while the others circled the table.

Mr. Mukesh: Hello Rishi

Rishi: Hello, uncle, where is Saru?

Mr. Mukesh: That's the question I was going to ask you. Did you guys fight again?

Mrs. Sharmila: Mukesh, don't get in between them; they are both devoted to each other, although they squabble all the time. Saru must be coming; I am coming from her room.

Mr. Mukesh: I totally get it. Last time, when these two didn't speak for a day, I interfered, and they ended up blaming me for the situation. I have learned my lesson not to meddle between them, Sharmila. By the way, Rishi, I just noticed that you look quite handsome and good without a mustache.

Rishi responded to his uncle's comment with a smile, but deep inside, he felt a sense of sadness about his behavior towards Saru. He realized that his words and actions had caused a rift between them, and he wished he could mend their relationship.

As the conversation continued, Saru, Mr. Mukesh, and Mr. Srinivas expressed and shared how their day was spent. Mrs. Sharmila and Mrs. Roja were completely engrossed in their respective gossip worlds. Saru seemingly avoided any direct interaction or eye contact with Rishi at the dinner table; despite Rishi's attempts to grab her attention through gestures and movements, Saru remained indifferent, focusing solely on her meal.

Rishi keenly observed Saru's facial expressions, deducing that she was upset with him. The atmosphere during dinner was tense, with an unspoken tension between Rishi and Saru, which affected the overall dynamics of the family gathering.

After the meal, as the family bid each other goodnight and prepared to depart, the unresolved issue between Rishi and Saru remained. The unspoken tension lingered, leaving Rishi feeling even more unsettled about their strained relationship.

After giving it some thought, Rishi decided to end their awkward silence by following Saru into her room.

Rishi: Hey, Saru!

Saru: What?

Rishi: I need to talk.

Saru: I'd rather not talk or discuss anything.

Rishi felt discouraged and disheartened when Saru did not show any interest in hearing from him. As he walked towards her room, following her, his steps were heavy. The sense of despondency was heightened when she did not respond to him when he called her again. Rishi slumped onto the floor as the weight of mixed emotions pressed him down. The sadness soaked into his being, rendering him motionless and immersed in a state of wretchedness.

Saru noticed he wasn't following her and turned to see him sitting with a gloomy and fearful expression. She returned to him, suppressing her anger, sat beside him, and inquired, "Rishi, say it."

Rishi: What?

Saru: The problem has been pounding your brain, tightening your heart, and compressing your stomach bag. I was aware that you were keeping something important from me.

Rishi cocked his chin and fixed his gaze squarely on hers. He seemed to open up and say something at that precise moment However, just as their bond was deepening, his phone abruptly rang, disrupting the atmosphere they had created. Rishi's phone began to ring. Rishi and Saru glanced at the screen simultaneously and discovered it was an incoming call from an unsaved and unfamiliar number. They both glanced at the screen and saw that it was a call from an unknown number. Rishi disregarded. He received another call from the same phone number. Rishi chose to ignore the call, but despite his dismissal, the same unfamiliar number rang repeatedly, instilling uncertainty and curiosity in the air.

Saru's worry grew as the unfamiliar number continued to ring repeatedly. Uncertainty filled the air, fueling her curiosity and heightening her concern.

Saru: You should attend it, Rishi.

Rishi: At this time, who would call me? There must be some misdialed numbers.

Saru: If someone calls you repeatedly, they must not be calling you accidentally. So you should answer. I will wait.

Rishi: Hmmm, Hello, who is this?

Sindhu: Hello, Rishi... Sobs. I am Sindhu, said the voice, trembling with fear.

Rishi: Sindhu, why are you crying? What happened? Whose number is this?

Sindhu continued to cry loudly.

Rishi: Sindhu, calm down. Where are you? Does someone say something?

Sindhu: Rishi, I arrived with some friends for a few drinks at this bar at around 8 o'clock, which is across from Dutt Island.

Rishi: Okay, but why are you frightened and crying?

Sindhu: A stranger from the crowd came over to my table as we were eating, lifted the food, and began to eat it, making us uncomfortable and disgusted. When we asked him to stop, he did more; when I shouted, he poured water on the food; and when my friend Saranya raised her hand, he tried to act rudely with her. After we begged him not to hurt her, he stopped, but the troublemaker persisted. What do you seek? Why are you bothering us? He stopped what he had been doing for a few minutes when I asked him, drew closer to me, tightened his hold on my hands, and said, "Tell Rishi to attend the calls." He then turned and gave me a horrifying look before leaving.

Rishi: What the devil?

When Rishi learned that the idiot had threatened Sindhu, his mind went blank, his skin turned clammy, and he was at a loss for words. He set the phone aside.

After noticing him, Saru took the phone. As she spoke with Sindhu, Saru recognized the image and handed the phone to Rishi, telling him to "talk to her," adding, "I think we should go there."

Rishi: I'm so sorry I put you in harm's way. Sindhu, where are you? Do your parents know about this?

Sindhu sobbed uncontrollably over the phone, her voice choked with grief. With a heavy heart, she reassured him that she would be fine because she was at home right now, accompanied by Saranya, and planned to spend the night at home, and Rishi assured her that he would meet Sindhu tomorrow at the crack of dawn.

Sindhu: Yeah, okay, but Rishi Who exactly is that? What is it about him that bothers you?

Rishi: You must be exhausted; eat something and then retire to bed. When we meet in person, I'll speak to you in person.

Sindhu: Well, good night, Rishi.

Rishi struggled to comprehend what had happened and how terrified she had become as a result of some obnoxious asshole threatening her in front of the horde.

Knowing he was picky and rarely ate at dinner, Saru bought some juice. When he refused to drink it or do anything else, Saru insisted and forced him to finish the entire glass.

Saru: Rishi, look at me and tell me everything you've been trying to keep from me while going through all of this alone.

Rishi: Hmmm…

Saru: Are you in danger?

Rishi: How do I begin? When I returned to my room the other day after a few drinks, I noticed a box with a cutely printed gift wrapper on the bed, and I assumed you had kept the box as a surprise. As we give gifts on our birthdays, I quickly rushed to open the box and was eager to see what was inside.

Saru pricked up her ears when Rishi continued to speak.

Rishi: Since the box was filled with pictures, I considered it a thoughtful gift, as I love clicking photos. As I began to look through each one, one photo caught my attention and sent a chill down my spine. It was an image of you, peacefully asleep. What startled me even more was the presence of numerous other photos featuring both you and me, taken from different angles in our respective rooms. It dawned on me that the sender of the box was not you, as I initially assumed.

Saru: Oh, my god. Why didn't you tell me about it? Anything else in the box?

Rishi: Hmm, there was a handwritten, folded note between the pictures.

Saru: What was mentioned on it?

Rishi: Is it love, or are you just drawn into a relationship? Let's say goodbye until the next surprise. Have a peaceful sleep, is written on it. I went straight to the window to check if someone might drop the box; all was clear. I came down to see near the entrance; when I opened the gate, it was clear again.

Suddenly, there was a scrabbling noise and a thud from the helper quarters, and when I strided towards the quarters, the door was closed and no lights were on. Then I turned to the other side; the watchman was nowhere to be seen. I called out for him, but there was no response. I then opened the gates to look, but all that was visible were wide, plain, noiseless, and humanless roads. When I turned and shut the gate a moment later, a car with its engine running suddenly appeared on the other side of the road. When I ran to investigate, the car that was parked there started speeding down the road. Due to the darkness, I couldn't see the details of the car, and I was feeling a bit tipsy.

Saru: Oh my God, this is terrifying me! Who is this sadist who wants to cause us trouble? But how did he manage to capture us at home on camera?

Rishi: I have no idea; nothing was mentioned on the cover, and the pictures were packaged in a normal cardboard box. He didn't stop there, either; the next was when we went to the salon together a few hours ago, and I got a text that said, "New makeover, not bad." The message I received immediately dampened my mood, and as we drove towards home, my phone rang several times. I didn't answer it willingly, as you were there beside me.

Saru: I can recall that and understand.

Rishi: Later, when I tried to call, the phone was off, and now he had reached Sindhu and threatened her.

Saru: With everything going on, it seemed like we were floundering in danger. Dammit. How could you be so calm? You weren't displaying any sort of action?

Rishi: As of now, we will wait for his next move. Oh, my lioness, please slow down. I admit that I needn't have worried this much if you weren't one of the targets in addition to me. So I decided to enlist the assistance of Raghu Ram's uncle.

Saru: There is nothing in this world that we cannot accomplish with the help of sharp minds and strong wills; whoever this person might be, he cannot harm us. But we must consider the potential consequences of involving the police. While seeking their assistance may seem like a logical course of action, it's essential to recognize the potential complications that could arise, like attracting unwanted attention, potentially resulting in a loss of privacy and freedom. The presence of constant surveillance could restrict our actions and impact our daily lives.

Rishi: clenched facial muscles and fists Well, I totally get what you said, but I can't wait for more to put us in danger.

Saru: Calm down; let's definitely call on his help when we need it. What if Uncle Raghav brought all of the information home? Parents wouldn't be able to handle it.

Rishi: Yeah, you are right, Saru. I haven't given it a thought. Our parents are overly sensitive, and their unwavering love for us will be overshadowed by fear. This will put us both in house jail, severely limit our ability to travel, and cause a slew of other problems in our daily lives.

Saru: In my head, I have the exact same recording. But don't worry; we'll figure something out. So, how do you feel now that you've shared with me? And please don't weave or braid animal examples into your response; just tell me something straight.

Rishi: took a deep and long breath. I deeply apologize for not immediately informing you about this disturbing discovery. I was maddened by the contents of the box and needed some time to process the situation before sharing it with you. Of course, now that I have shared the baggage that I have been carrying for a few days, I feel calm, like when an agitated bird kept in a small, cramped cage is released.

Saru: Ugh, again, you respond with an animal example. You won't change.

Rishi: Ignoring that, what do we do now? Saru ? Although what the idiot had done to Sindhu was intense, how did he manage to take photos of us?

Saru: Shit, a traitor on the inside? Someone may have been keeping an eye on us, or they may have fixed the miniature spy cameras. This someone could have been anyone who had recently visited the house.

Rishi: But how do we know? The house has been visited by a large number of people in the last few days because we hosted a party to celebrate your birthday and my engagement announcement, which was followed by a cocktail party near the pool, so the guest list is long.

Saru: The guest list isn't very long because there was a private party that limited the number of attendees. During lunch with the aunts and uncles, the majority of them were in the hallway. Later, a cocktail party was held near the pool, preventing anyone from getting inside our homes.

Rishi: What if someone from the crowd approached our rooms during lunch? Isn't that a possibility?

Saru: could be, because only our close relatives know where our rooms are; they must spend time in them for at least fifteen to twenty minutes to fix a camera at multiple random spots.

Rishi: Since the party took place at your house and mine might be locked, let's assume it was a relative, but they must have installed cameras in both of our rooms. It implies that someone has gained access to both houses.

Saru: But I don't think any of our relatives have; they're blameless and harmless, and the majority of the time they're engaged in gossiping, talking about jewelry, and specifically hunting the brides and bridegrooms for their sons and daughters.

Rishi: Then who? Who ? Before he or she causes harm to us, we should stop.

Saru: Indeed, when you go meet Sindhu tomorrow, I'll accompany you.

Rishi: Okay.

Saru: Rishi, it's too late; you need to go. We'll check the guest list tomorrow; perhaps we'll find something.

Rishi nodded and began walking down the hallway toward the house, his determination clear in his stride. Saru stood there, watching him leave, her worry evident in her furrowed brow. Without hesitation, she started running after him, their footsteps echoing through the empty hallway.

As they finally caught up with each other, Rishi turned to Saru and asked, "Are you worried?"

Saru paused for a moment, catching her breath, before responding, "Yes, I am. The situation is daunting."

Rishi took her hand in his, offering comfort and reassurance. " "So am I," he admitted, his voice filled with sincerity. They found a spot against the wall and sat down, their backs supported by its solid presence. They held onto each other tightly, finding solace in their shared embrace.

With a determined look in her eyes, Saru spoke up, her voice steady. "Let's navigate this storm together, like sailors on a ship. We will face this hardship bravely, anchoring ourselves to each other."

Rishi looked back into her eyes, his gaze filled with unwavering resolve. Yes, he replied, a hint of a smile forming on his lips. Let's sail the ship, fearlessly charting our course through whatever comes our way.

And in that moment, their intertwined hands held not only strength but also a profound sense of unity, and Rishi remained silent.

Saru: what? Dumb. You wouldn't do that?

Rishi: I certainly would, Saru. We are for each other.

Saru releases a slight smile from the corners of her lower lip, holds his hand more tightly, and says, "In hell and heaven."

Rishi: I can't sleep, as my heart is heavy. Before he does something bad, we should catch him, Saru.

Saru: Hmm… Yes, tell me something. Are you happy?

Rishi: Of course not; I'm terrified of what this person might do to you and Sindhu.

Saru: Do not attempt to be intelligent. Do you enjoy her company?

Rishi chose to be silent and had his face buried in his hands.

Saru: I know that you will remain silent, Rishi. You need to be happy because this is a lifetime commitment; don't give up on yourself for someone you don't care about and don't love.

Rishi: Have you lost your mind? Why would I give my life for someone I don't love? Of course, I care about Sindhu.

Saru: Yeah, your brain has stopped functioning properly, Rishi. I am aware that, despite your care, you do not love her.

Rishi: You said this for what reason?

Saru: Rishi, it's very obvious; I don't see the affectionate spark in your eyes, and those who are smitten tend to have a distinct, dreamy aura that envelops them in their own little world of romance. In fact, you try to blend in, put on phony smiles and plastic performances like a few crazy influencers to hike their follower counts, and act like you're moving around to attend some important business when in reality there will be nothing to do. Isnt?

Rishi: You are right, Saru.

Saru: Dumbo, then why are you getting engaged to her?

Rishi: Saru, she loves me, as I already said.

Saru: Rishi, but you don't love her.

Rishi: yelled, I don't love her, but what do I do? I didn't even kiss her; I never had any feelings for her. You know what? It really grinds my gears when I see her.

Saru: Then, why did you coerce yourself into making a false commitment?

Rishi: You should know how I was wired for this false commitment. When you were in Bangalore, I got to attend the alumni gathering. The alumni center was where I met Sindhu; seeing all of them after so many years made me nostalgic.

Few of us walked the halls, visited classrooms, and explored the entire campus, as everyone was emotional and happy to meet each other. Wamsi later joined us because his flight was delayed, and he was late due to that. Members of our group dispersed as they had to meet some other friends, and a few left for lunch, leaving me and Wamsi. While we were discussing everything from our early years to the present, Sindhu crossed our path as we were both heading to lunch. "Seeing her, you were the reason to miss this beauty," Wamsi said, and I was startled to hear it, Saru, and I questioned, "What are you saying, Wamsi? How could I be the reason for this?" He replied, "Hasn't she proposed to me yet?"

"Why would she?" I replied to him with a surprisingly shocked expression.

Wamsi responded, "What? When I flew to Bangalore for work three weeks ago, in movies, our seats were next to each other—what a coincidence, right? After a little chat, I was called for a club weekend, as she told me her stay would be for a month.

So why would I pass up an opportunity to meet a stunning woman? I've had a crush on her since we were students. I was introduced to a handsome man and a hot girl as her cousins, who were tagged along with Sindhu. We had a great time, and because the drinks had an effect on me, I proposed to her. To my surprise, she politely declined my proposal and stated that she was in love with someone else. I tried my luck, assuming she was already engaged, and when I contacted her to learn more about that lucky guy, I was amazed to learn your name."

I was shocked and responded to him, "Have you gone insane? My mind is still reeling from what you said. After school, I am seeing her today."

Wamsi: Come on, dude, be a little serious.

Rishi: Hey Wamsi, why would I joke about something that was connected to a woman?

Wamsi: Hmm, then she could propose to you today. Oh my God, what have I done? I shouldn't have revealed everything.

Rishi: As Wamsi caused chaos that I didn't care about, I took it as a sign and fled from Wamsi.

Saru: "So much had happened; why didn't you take a moment to share it with me?"

Rishi: "Please wait while I finish the mess, because it hasn't just happened. Anyway, now I'm saying it right."

Saru: "Okay, I'm paying attention."

Rishi: As everyone gathered for lunch, Sindhu immediately approached me with a cheery smile. In front of everyone, she gave me a peck on the cheek, placed a sweet in my mouth, and then quickly left the area. I lost it. I couldn't speak in front of friends who were only vaguely aware of Wamsi's story because I was in some sort of shock over what she had done in front of them. I just left the area in search of her, getting misunderstood and humiliated in front of friends instead of saying anything or reacting.

I went everywhere on campus in search of her, then received a call from the number. I answered, "Hi, Rishi, I am Sindhu speaking; are you searching for me?" I replied, Sindhu, What exactly did you do? Why ? and she replied, "Hey, Rishi, cool down." "Come to the parking space, car no. 5544," and she hangs up the call.

When I arrived at the parking space, I heard someone approaching the car from behind. As I turned back to see the person, I felt pain in the neck, like an ant bite. After that, I don't remember anything until I awoke a few hours later and realized I was in a luxurious room filled with pricey items that sparkled as if they had just been bought, in a clean, well-kept environment with no signs of humans. My body ached for a few minutes, and I searched for some water to quench my parched throat. As each second passed, the dry feeling in my throat got worse. My eyes noticed a glass of water that had been set on the side of the bed as I attempted to get out of bed.

I heard someone opening the door as I took minuscule steps to reach the table opposite the wall-mounted bed. I was stunned and shocked to see Sindhu joyfully approaching me. I couldn't stop my anger and frustration, so I lost control over all my senses and yelled at her.

Saru: Whatttt?

Rishi: Yes, Saru. When she opened her tear ducts, I felt bad and expressed my apologies. Sindhu recounted, gently wiping away her tears. Through sniffles, she managed to utter, "It's alright; it's you, Rishi, and I belong to you."

I completely ignored her words as I gained consciousness and observed my surroundings for clues about her whereabouts. "Where am I?" and "What happened to me?" Denying my questions, she urged me to prioritize my nourishment and requested that I eat something first.

My frustration grew, and I yelled, Have you lost your mind? Where are my belongings? I need my phone." Sindhu reassured me, "My things are safe with her, and she has proposed to me to have something to eat." "I once again denied inquiring about my phone, as I wanted to call home, and questioned her about the reason for my condition."

Sindhu responded, "Rishi, you approached my car while we were on the phone. As you came closer, you suddenly lost your balance and fell to the ground." I was filled with worry, and I immediately contacted a doctor, seeking reassurance about your well-being. The doctor's response eased my concern and assured me that you are perfectly fine. And I thought it would be best to bring you to my house so you could rest and recover.

We were both talking when we were interrupted by a tall man in his sixties, firm and wrinkled but energetic for his age, with a bright smile. Mr. Murthy, Sindhu's father, greeted me with, Hello, young man, so you are Rishi.

Yes, sir, I am Rishi. With trepidation, I wished him well and thanked him for looking after me.

Mr. Murthy: Well, young man, don't mention it. When my daughter spilled the beans about you two lovebirds, I was like, "Hold your horses, lady!" But dang, when I heard about your family, I was all like, "Yeehaw, saddle up!" Her decision has made me feel as proud as a peacock, and I am confident that by becoming a member of your family, my daughter will receive the highest level of respect and love. I accidentally ran into Mr. Srinivas at the business party a few months ago, and I'll be seeing him again in a few days to talk to him about you guys.

His words nearly knocked me out once more. Sindhu cut his father's words like a bypass; he retained a humorous manner, and after a while, he left the room. I eyed her with all the cold loathing I felt for the way I was introduced to her dad. Shortly after getting my things from her, I passed everyone in their house and eventually came to the road. I then remembered that my car was in the school parking lot, though after denying it, she insisted that her driver drive me home.

Saru: When did this all happen, Rishi?

Rishi: I told you, you weren't here in Vizag for two weeks when you flew to Bangalore with your parents.

Saru: I have noticed a change in your behavior since I returned, and it's been bothering me. I have tried to get answers by asking and teasing you, but you have kept silent. It's been weighing heavily on my mind, and I am feeling distraught and upset about it.

Rishi didn't utter a word, and his gaze was fixed on Saru's eyes, conveying a deep sense of sorrow.

Saru: Why couldn't you call and tell me everything when I was in Bangalore? Anyway, we'll get to that later. What happened next?

Rishi: I was in a strange, off-putting frame of mind when I got home that day after attempting to sleep through the night in an effort to regain composure, but my thoughts wouldn't let me close my eyelids. Since Sindhu was the only person present when I lost consciousness, I couldn't help but feel a sense of suspicion and intrigue about what might have occurred that day. I couldn't shake off the nagging suspicion that she might have had something to do with my sudden collapse.

The next morning, although I didn't want to meet her, I had no choice because she hadn't intentionally given me back my card wallet. When she suggested we meet the following evening at a restaurant, I agreed to go in order to learn the truth behind her lies, control my rage, and try to come to an amicable agreement by offering an olive branch.

Details were described in the text she sent me when I arrived at one of the city's upscale hotels and was seated. My gut kept alerting me to leave the area before I became entangled in yet another web of trouble. As I listened and showed some respect for my inner callings, I stood up to leave before she arrived. I saw her arrive for a split second, which put me in a tizzy.

I questioned her angrily, "Why did you do this?" without offering any polite greetings. Sindhu exhibited her fake or naive smiley behavior to me, which was creepy, as she came close to me and whispered, "Get ready to get thrilled, and my respects to them."

Before I could even utter "What?" The word returned to the voice box before resonating in space, stopping the vibration of my vocal cords, which create a voice.

Saru: inquisitively, Who are they?

Rishi: "Parents." Every cell in my body reacted in shock at the sight of my parents, and I couldn't help but wonder what they were thinking when they saw me with Sindhu.

Saru: Oh, my god! I can empathize with your experience of feeling shocked upon seeing your parents. It's understandable how that situation would have elicited such a strong reaction.

Rishi: I took a few deep breaths and opened my mouth to say, "Hi, dad, and mom." I stood there looking into their eyes for a reply, while Sindhu went to my parents, greeted them well, and she said, "I bought the wallet that you forgot at home and left," which planted seeds of doubt in my parents' minds.

After she left, as we were facing each other in silence, the waiter placed two cups of cappuccinos with heart symbols on them, which I didn't order. This action resembles pouring water on a seed that is in doubt.

I couldn't ask her to stay or for me to leave in front of my parents because of the situation I was in. As you might expect, my mother spent the next hour interrogating and inspecting me as she stirred the cream with a plunger until the butterfat separated from the buttermilk. To make matters worse, Sindhu's parents suddenly appeared at the table.

Saru: Wait, what? Why did Sindhu's parents come?

Rishi: Hmm, yeah, and more twists are coming. Be patient and wait it out, Saru.

Saru: I don't think it was just a random visit from Sindhu's parents; I'm sure Sindhu's mind was behind this invasion.

Rishi: "Hey Rishi, what a small world!" "Are you by yourself, or did Sindhu come with you? Mr. Murthy said this with a happy face and a happy tone, while Mrs. Murthy stood next to him with a neutral expression."

With an additional dose of shock, my lips were sealed. While I struggled to open my mouth, Dad and Mr. Murthy introduced themselves independently.

I was on edge, tensing up as they talked, because I was worried about what would happen if Mr. Murthy actually revealed the truth about my unimaginable, unplanned stay at their house. Thankfully, he didn't mention anything about my stay, which was definitely a relief and better than a sharp blow to the teeth.

Saru listened attentively to the Rishi with a curious mindset and inquired about what happened next in an inquisitive tone.

Rishi: Sindhu's mini-show completely persuaded my parents, especially my dad, and the following sunrise brought the worst news of my life. Remember, at the first rain of the season, Mr. Murthy confirmed the exchange of the rings.

You're right, Saru. I was too timid to approach Dad and engage him in conversation. In any case, what was there to say, Saru? and to break off the engagement after our families agreed that we were in a committed relationship. Even if I speak with them, they won't believe me; in addition, they see this as a business transaction because we will augment more capital gains. However, now that parents have given their word to them, honoring that commitment holds great significance for our parents, and their pride is deeply intertwined with this promise, and I am unwilling to compromise or diminish their pride in any way.

Saru: This is a grave situation. What you experienced was disconcerting; how could someone do this? No doubt, Sindhu is a troublemaker. Did you look into her background?

Rishi: Just a troublemaker? Nah, she must be more like the person who is happy when someone is in pain; she is impulsive and displays more aggressive psychic behavior. I tried checking her past; it's like whenever I try to make a move against her, she comes to know, and in return, she blocks me back by doing so in such a way that you can't even imagine how far she would extend to do anything.

Saru: We need to start resolving this issue right away and call off the engagement. This is horrifying, and I'm so sorry; you must be so stressed out juggling with so many issues.

As Saru shared her emotions, tears streamed down her face, and Rishi approached her and cared to wipe her tears. He embraced her with a deep and powerful emotional intensity, and she responded in kind; eventually, she freed herself from his arms. Rishi suggested that it was nearly two in the morning and advised that they should get some rest and visit Sindhu's house in the first blush of the morning.

While Rishi was walking home, an overwhelming feeling of unease overcame him as he made his way back to his house because he thought he could feel a shadowy figure following him up the stairs. He continued taking a few more steps, ignoring the feeling of unease. But as the emotion grew stronger and took control, he suddenly turned around to discover an empty, eerily silent area in front of him. He let out a sigh and went to his room.

Despite their brief slumber, it was restorative and deep, as they had spent the majority of the night conversing and disclosing their deepest thoughts and feelings to each other, particularly Rishi's agony. Both of them had high hopes that they would discover a solution to their problems.

As the next day arrived, a new dawn broke, illuminating the fresh and vibrant rays of sunlight.

After finishing their morning chores, they met for breakfast. Saru noticed Rishi coming nearer to the table and gave him a radiant smile, and she informed Sita to bring an egg sandwich with more tomato slices and steer clear of mayonnaise, as well as a slice of bread with peanut butter spread.

With a beaming smile, Rishi expressed gratitude to Saru, praising her choice and the satisfying meal that would fill his stomach. Rishi bit off a chunk of his peanut butter-topped slice of bread as Sita presented him with the personalized breakfast.

Mrs.Sharmila: There was a full house at the table. Did you see these two, Mukesh? I advised against interfering because they had argued the night before and were now showing each other love and care.

Mr. Mukesh: Oh, I see. It's nice to see them making up and putting their differences aside for a moment. That's the spirit of family gatherings, isn't it?

Mrs.Sharmila: Bringing the entire family together can either be an ice breaker or an ice maker, depending on how things go, but in the case of these two, they fight and speedily return at least once a day.

Mrs. Roja: Why are you two not together?

Mrs. Roja's question hung in the air, causing everyone to abruptly pause in their actions, as if the earth stopped spinning for a moment. Considering her statement, Mr. Srinivas, deeply affected, set aside his food and fixed a penetrating gaze on Mrs. Roja. He couldn't help but comment on the noticeable change in Mrs. Roja's behavior and words since Rishi's engagement to Sindhu was announced. It appeared as though Roja harbored a hidden resistance to the impending engagement.

Apologizing for her earlier phrasing, Mrs. Roja clarified her inquiry, emphasizing the recent fight between Rishi and Saru and their subsequent separation. Tension laced her voice, indicating her genuine concern.

While the minor drama unfolded, Rishi and Saru exchanged glances and grinned internally. Meanwhile, the other members of the family seem to remain captivated yet bewildered, as if watching an unknown language movie without subtitles. Undeterred by the unresolved tensions, the rest of the group continued to eat, attempting to maintain a sense of normalcy despite the lingering unease.

As everyone departed, Mrs. Roja stayed, thinking intently while clutching a steaming mug of coffee. Meanwhile, Sita observed Saru and Rishi fleeing before drawing the attention of their family.

Savoring the scalding hot coffee, Mrs. Roja's thoughts churned, and she finally voiced her inquiry, "Where have Rishi and Saru disappeared to?"

Sita, amused, couldn't help but respond with a chuckle, concealing her face behind a kitchen napkin. "Those adorable love birds took off a while ago," she replied.

Mrs. Roja, offering some advice, remarked, "If you are done playing the role of shy spectator and prying into other people's private lives, it's time to focus on your own tasks.

Acknowledging the remark, Sita swiftly made her way back to the kitchen, responding with a respectful "Okay, Madam."

Mrs. Roja noticed Sita walk into the kitchen and speak in hushed tones, as if only she could hear her, "Hmm, glad. At least Sita's brain is functioning and thinking like a normal human being. I don't understand why others can't see the pure love between them; learning string theory is not required to understand it; an average brain is enough."

As Rishi and Saru stepped out of the house and got into the vehicle to meet Sindhu, Rishi's phone buzzed with a message from Sindhu. Upon reading the message, Rishi's face turned blue, prompting him to say, "Speak of the Devil."

Noticing him, Saru teased him by saying, "Why does your facial celebration of joy suddenly turn into a grim and gloomy ghost town?" However, Rishi chose to maintain silence, offering no response to Saru's playful comment.

Saru: Something important? What's in the message? Is the message from the troublemaker?

Rishi: Yes, she has asked me to arrive early at home for a surprise.

Saru: Rishi, What did you type in response?

Rishi: I haven't yet; what should I reply with?

Saru: Okay, but why are you sweltering like it's the middle of summer?

Rishi: Definitely, her surprises are horrifying, intense, and extreme as she plays with our emotions. So how can I be as calm as the blue sea when everything around me is roiling?

Saru: Relax; let's see what she has planned for you.

After enjoying a delightful ride that lasted for a few minutes, Rishi and Saru made their way to Sindhu's house entrance. Upon entering the hall of house,

They were greeted by the sight of Sindhu happily watching a cooking show. They witnessed her enthusiasm, which triggered a shift in Saru and Rishi's thoughts.

Rishi: Hi Sindhu,

Sindhu: Hey, Rishi, oh my god, Saraswati is here.

Saru: Hey Sindhu, I'm sorry for showing up without informing you.

Rishi: You two converse, and let some show the way to the washroom, Sindhu.

Sindhu acknowledged Rishi's request and promptly summoned Ramu, instructing him about the situation: "Ramu, assist Rishi and show him the way to the restroom." Ramu nodded his head and said, "Yes, sir, please come along with me." Sindhu turned and attended Saru.

Sindhu: Come on, Saru, no need for formalities; we are friends and soon to be a family. What would you like to have?

With a forced and fake smile, Saru declined Sindhu's offer of food or drink, quickly transitioning into the topic of the previous night's incident. She said, I am sorry about what happened last night. How are you feeling now?

Sindhu, attempting to conceal her underlying happiness, adopted a somber expression and responded, "Well, what can I say, Saru? The man at the restaurant was completely out of line, behaving inappropriately towards a woman. Thankfully, my friends were there, and he eventually left without causing any physical harm. I considered contacting the police, but he warned me not to involve anyone, as it could lead to harm for Rishi. So, I didn't do anything against him.

Saru: It's unfortunate and saddening to hear about the distressing situation you encountered at the restaurant last night. As an aside, can you identify the man? What if we go to the pub and check the footage?

Upon hearing Saru's words, Sindhu's senses alerted, and her throat parched and looked uptight. Leaving Saru there, Sindhu turned right and made her way to the nearby massive oval shaped dinner table. It stood proudly in the center of the room, crafted expertly from dark, luxurious wood, and it radiated an aura of refinement and elegance. There, she poured herself a glass of water, taking a sip before attempting to open her phone to send a text.

Saru approached quietly, leaned in, and peered in, curious about what Sindhu was doing with her phone. Saru suddenly moved closer to Sindhu's right ear, startling her. She quickly pressed the home screen button on her phone while firmly holding it in her left palm. With a composed demeanor, Sindhu responded, "Oh sure, why don't you have some juice?"

Saru: No, dear, I am good with plain water. Uff, where was I? Yeah, footage; if you recognize the person, we can enlist the help of the police to catch him and teach him a lesson.

Sindhu: You are correct, but...

Saru: But what exactly? Why did you pause? Are you scared to get caught?

Sindhu: Excuse me, Saru.

Saru: I mean, are you scared that the person might hurt you?

Sindhu: I am fearless, and I come from a valiant family. I'll go to any length to get what I want, but why get involved before the ring ceremony? When the ceremony is over, I'll notify Dad and make sure everything is in order. My father will make a big mess if he finds out about this, and it will be widely covered in the media.

Rishi: Sorry, it took time. Sindhu, I am so sorry for last night; I put you in danger. How does he look? What else did he say? By the way, where is your friend?

Sindhu: Hmmmm, with a face like a fiddle. I tried to make out his features in the dim DJ lighting. He seemed tall, but it was difficult to distinguish his exact appearance. My friend, Saranya, departed in the early morning hours as she boarded a flight for some business. I am glad to say that I'm safe and well. Let's move on from any negative experiences and focus on the exciting surprises ahead.

As Saru observed Sindhu's dramatic narrator of nonsense, Rishi said, "Sindhu, I am sorry once more for putting you in danger and continuously bringing up those unpleasant memories."

Sindhu: Okay, okay, leave it, Rishi. So, are you ready to be blown away?

Rishi muttered to himself, "You wouldn't leave me if I said no, so it's better to act excited."

Sindhu: What exactly did you say?

Rishi: I said, I am so excited to know what you brought to surprise me.

With boisterous laughter, Sindhu handed him cover. Curiosity piqued, Rishi pondered, "Hmm, it feels heavy. What could be concealed within this cover?" He carefully grasped it.

Sindhu, wearing a wide smile that revealed all her teeth from molar to molar, encouraged him and said, "Just open it and find out, Rishi."

Upon opening the package, he discovered an array of elegant and costly wedding invitations. The sight of cards caused his heart to race with agitation. Rishi tried to put on a happy face like others do when they get to see their own wedding invitation, but he failed to do so, and he could feel his pulse accelerate as memories of past surprises with her flooded his mind.

Sindhu: See, I told you you would be excited.

Rishi: feigned it, Yeah, Sindhu, but why the rush when we have yet to engage?

Sindhu: I am eager for our wedding and want to ensure everything is flawless. Because made-to-order invitations take a long time to manufacture, they must be ordered well in advance to avoid delays.

Saru was seething with anger, which intensified with each passing second as she witnessed Sindhu's exceptional acting skills that could rival those of an Oscar winner. Determined to put an end to it, Saru confronted Rishi with an air of assertiveness, saying he could depart immediately. Catching Saru's unspoken demand for his exit, he sprang into action and smartly activated their contingency plan. Rishi explained the urgency of a matter that required his immediate departure.

Sindhu: You have just arrived, and now you are talking about leaving already? Why are you planning to go so soon? Perhaps you could consider staying for lunch?

Rishi: I am sorry to upset you, but I have to go, Sindhu.

Sindhu: What's up with Rishi's quick coming and going? What's with the solemn expression? Is he planning to take over the world, or has he discovered a new planet?

Saru: Haha, it looks like you are about to start a spy mission on him. The thing is, Rishi's father arranged a meeting with clients from abroad, so his attendance is required. I can keep you company for a little while if you are okay with my presence.

Sindhu: Huh. Work beacons cannot be ignored. Of course, you should please stay here so we can have some girl time.

Saru: Awesome. I am all for it.

Sindhu: Well, despite being classmates and sitting at separate desks in different sections, we didn't exactly hit it off. But now I am about to become a permanent fixture in your family.

Saru: Haha, it appears that our distant friendship between classmates in different classes is about to become much closer! Better start practicing those forced family photo smiles.

Sindhu: You are a funny person, Saru. I can already feel the love and warmth radiating from this impending union.

Saru: Hmm, so what now? Got any plans? How about giving me a home tour?

Unease radiated from Sindhu, and she uttered the words, "Sure, Sure." She was reluctant to reveal the house; she was visibly hesitant. She suggested beginning with the upstairs floor, acknowledging the presence of exterior stairs, which offered more privacy.

"Sindhu madam, madam, Sonu babu has been trying to reach you for the past 30 minutes, and as you didn't answer, he even called the home number," the helper from inside rushed to say.

As the helper approached, she conveyed in a low tone, "Sonu Babu's voice indicated that the situation was important, and he sounded anguished."

Sindhu: Thank you for letting me know, Radha. I will call Sonu back immediately and see what the matter is. And Saru, please continue with the upstairs tour, and I will join you as soon as I can.

As Sindhu hurriedly whirled inside, her movements displayed a sense of urgency.

Various questions raced through Saru's mind as she observed Sindhu's reaction. "Who might be Sonu?" "Why does she tremble at the mere mention of his name, as if she has encountered a fearsome reptile?" Realizing the need for more information, Saru contemplated the idea of delving deeper into the matter and the mystery surrounding Sonu, all while striking the stairs.

While she continued to step up the next stair, the helper caught up with her, offering assistance. Sensing Saru's curiosity, the helper gently interjected, "Allow me to guide you, madam."

As Saru said ok to the helper, someone from below called out "Radha. Radha." as they ascended the stairs, requesting that she attend Sindhu as she requested.

As soon as Radha heard this, she abruptly left Saru and made her way down the stairs with a quick step that was reminiscent of Rajinikanth's signature gait.

Saru smiled at the sight of Radha's mannerisms and thought there was something exaggeratedly theatrical about her.

Alerting her senses, Saru wasted no time and quickly made her way to the floor. The floor consisted of a line of two rooms and two opposite rooms, all of which had closed doors with a number lock system installed. She attempted to push the first one, but it failed. Then she moved to an adjacent room, but it also remained locked. Eventually, she tried the first door on the other side, and it opened. Silently, Saru entered the room and quickly deduced that it was Sindhu's parents' bedroom. She left the room without making any noise and tried the next door. Fortunately, the door was opened. Upon seeing the multiple photo frames on the plain wall, everything from newborn to recently framed, including pre-framed photos of family members too, Saru realized that it was Sindhu's room. She quickly clicked all the photos and checked the drawers, the wardrobe, and everything else.

While walking on the carpet, Saru felt something underneath it and lifted it to discover a few gift wrapper cuttings. As she knelt to pick them up, she heard footsteps and quickly replaced the carpet as it was before, the footsteps drawing closer. Quickly, she headed towards the floor's entrance.

Saru wiped the sweat from her temples with her sleeves and tried to relax her face, but she felt tense at the sound of the approaching footsteps, which were louder and sharper.

Saru had difficulty masking her nervousness and often failed. It seemed for one instant as if the move had been a failure, though taking risks, However, when she saw and heard the helper singing a song from a movie starring Mega Star, she relaxed her tense muscles and joined her voice with Radha.

Radha: grinning bashfully, You sing really well, madam.

Saru: Haha, nah, you sing really well. Where did you learn?

Radha: Well, blow me down, madam. You must have misunderstood me completely. I am a certified graduate of the prestigious seventh grade in my village! I may not be the sharpest tool in the shed, but I can read like a pro. You see, life around here can be a real snooze-fest. I am stuck in this house all day with no one to chat with, and as a jack of all trades, I have to do a million tasks. So, to inject some excitement into my life, I turn to my trusty singing videos before bed. They are like my personal concert every night.

Saru: I am sorry to hear that you feel lonely here, Radha. It was lovely meeting you, and I must say that I find you to be a charming and humorous young lady.

Radha: giggled. Oh, my Buddha, the matter that I wanted to convey to you—I forgot that.

Saru: Oh, what's that?

Radha: Sindhu Madam is currently busy. She has asked you to come down and take a seat in the hall, as she will join you shortly, within a few minutes.

Saru: All right, let's go down, Radha.

Radha: Grinning. Follow me, madam.

They were moving when Saru's phone buzzed with the text message. It was Rishi when she looked at her phone. "Anything suspicious? Enough detective work; now get out of there and head home. I have been out for some work; I will be home in an hour."

"Haha, that's not funny with an annoyed face emoji, and once I get home, I'll tell you in detail." Saru replied, and she kept the phone in her bag as Radha watched her closely, her eyes wide with curiosity and the urge to ask.

Saru: Sorry, want to say something? Radha

Radha: Yes, madam...

Saru: What is it?

Radha: You typed the message so quickly. Just to send "good morning" as a message, I usually spend a minute searching for and typing each letter. I wish I was able to type the message as quickly as you. I also wish my father would put me in a good school, or at least continue my education. You might have seen kids crying and showing tantrums to attend school, which was a complete backpedal in my case.

Saru: I am so sorry to know this. Is there any way to help you? Just let me know if you are interested in rejoining the school.

Radha: That's kind of you, but I can't study now. For my parents, I have reached a point in my life where I am ready to get married, and my parents have already arranged a marriage for me. But I was reluctant to go through with the wedding, and the groom's parents were also demanding a dowry that my parents couldn't afford. My parents had to send me away from them as an only child to try and collect some money to meet the dowry requirements with a distant cousin.

Saru: That is very unfortunate; there is no set age at which we can do the things we enjoy. Just let me know if you're interested in furthering your education.

Radha: Thank you so much, madam.

Saru exchanged a warm smile with Radha and shared her phone number. and she stated, "I must take my leave now, and please inform Sindhu."

Reacting quickly, Radha pleaded, "Please wait for Sindhu madam to arrive; otherwise, she might reprimand me for letting you go."

Saru assured Radha, saying, "I will leave her a message. I wouldn't want to trouble you in any way."

Expressing gratitude, Radha acknowledged Saru's understanding, saying, "I appreciate your understanding, and I thank you. Once Sindhu Madam arrives, I will inform her about your departure. It was nice meeting you, Radha," Saru retorted with a big smile. Regarding Sindhu's parents, I don't see them.

Radha: Ooh, well, it's so difficult to comprehend the house, its regulations, and the people residing in it. Murthy sir is like the husband, who is always at the office and working, and Rajani madam is living her life in Bangalore with her nephew, Sonu sir. If you don't spill the tea, I'll tell you what my coworkers tattle all the time.

Saru: Radha, your secret will be safe with me.

Radha: Previously, this family was full of warmth and affection; however, tragedy has struck them with a cruel and unforgiving hand. The family had been dealt a devastating blow when Rajani Madam's beloved brother and sister-in-law were killed in a car accident. Sonu sir, who had already been through the agony of losing his parents, is now in the care of Rajani ma'am, who has taken on the responsibility of her dearest nephew.

Ah, I couldn't believe what I was witnessing now. Sonu sir and Sindhu madam are tight. Every time Sonu Sir called, Sindhu Madam would disappear into a world of her own, talking for hours on end. It was as if no one existed in the home. So, everyone in the house speculated that they were a couple and would soon tie the knot, but something else was brewing. Oh Lord, why did you entangle me in this house? Radha exclaimed helplessly, letting out a sigh.

Saru felt that this information, which she pulled out of Radha with less effort, would certainly help them, and she thought that Radha's daily activities were dominated by watching movies, which suggested a potential overinfluence and might wrongly suggest the closeness among them and not jump to conclusions.

Saru smiled at Radha and bid farewell to her, and as she walked out of the house, a vehicle of hers was parked outside. She noticed a man in uniform standing nearby, talking on the phone. Curious, she walked over to the car and saw that there was no familiar driver. She approached the man and inquired, "Newly appointed?"

Driver: Yes, madam.

Saru hastily settled into the back seat of the car while the driver quickly started the engine. Saru messaged Rishi, "I started home, and Thank you for sending the car." She spent her travel time scrolling through Instagram, catching up on a few reels at her leisure.

The driver kept a close eye on Saru in the rearview mirror, and whenever Saru caught him looking, he averted his gaze suspiciously and repeated the act.

Saru noticed but said nothing. They reached the home, and the driver opened the door for Saru. Before she took a step forward, she turned around and asked his name.

With no expression on his face, he uttered, "Raju Madam." Saru advised him to keep his focus on the steering wheel and the road. She turned away from him. As she walked into her room, she remembered her desire for a refreshing glass of orange juice to combat the heat, but she refused to drink or eat anything at Sindhu's home as Rishi had instructed. He walked into the kitchen to retrieve it, and she was taken aback to find the car driver busy wrapping the covers of the boxes while Sita arranged sweets within.

Saru, with a weird feeling and a slightly elevated tone, questioned the driver, "What brings you here?"

Sita: As per Sharmila madam's instructions, I called the driver, Raju, inside to send the sweet boxes to the designated houses mentioned in the list.

Saru: Oh, get me a glass of orange juice, the way I take it.

Sita: Yeah, Saru di freshly squeezed oranges, leaving the pulp intact and refraining from added sugars. Consider it done in two minutes.

Raju completely ignored Saru's presence and continued to work. After instructing Sita to send her juice to her room, Saru made a move to leave the kitchen. However, she hesitated and turned back, pulling a chair and sitting down while keeping a watchful eye on the driver. In a suspicious tone, she asked, "Sita, where is this weird smell coming from?"

Sita went on a sniffing spree, trying to catch the scent of something strange in the air. After a minute of vigorous nasal training, she realized that the smell was actually that of champak flowers. Albeit not fresh ones, it was not at all strange. She even speculated that someone might have doused themselves in Champak perfume.

Saru heard Sita's comment about the strong smell of champak and realized it might be coming from the driver. "Oh no, not champak again! That smell gives me a headache." She gave him a sharp look and waited for his response, hoping that he would say something or leave the area as early as he could.

The driver remained silent, grabbed the sweets and the list, and bolted from the scene like he had a sudden urge to run a marathon. However, Sita wasn't about to let him get away that easily, and she yelled after him,

Sita: Hey, buddy! There's no need to take a full-on Champak perfume bath. Just a spritz or two will do, okay?

Raju: Oh, sorry, I didn't realize that smell was bothering you.

Sita: It looks like the driver needs a little discipline and a change of perfume, and Saru di, Did he behave poorly toward you?

Saru: Oh, definitely! A new perfume for him would be a relief, so we don't have to endure the unpleasant smell. By the way, why did you make that comment? Sita.

Sita: I noticed that you seemed bothered by his presence.

Saru: True, Sita, it looks like we've got ourselves a real-life version of the creepy chauffeur from a horror movie. I mean, I've never seen this guy before in my life, but he's probably been lurking in the shadows, waiting to pounce on unsuspecting passengers. And those looks he gave me in the car? Let's just say that if looks could kill, I'd be gone by now. But seriously, Sita. Who picked up this shady character?

Sita: Yeah, Saru di, he is creepy; his appearance is beyond description; he's also been doused in the Champak perfume river, as you so aptly put it; and he was subsequently appointed as a temporary replacement for a driver named Ramesh.

Mukesh Sir made the decision after Ramesh became ill and requested a replacement until he recovered.

Saru: Okay, then Just be careful, Sita.

Saru had finished her juice and was on her way back to her room when she noticed the driver standing around the corner. They exchanged glances, but neither of them wanted to speak. As she walked, she had the distinct impression that something about the driver was off.

Rishi: Hey, Saru.

Saru: Hey there, speed racer! Finally made it through the traffic, huh?

Rishi: Haha, you got me! It seems like the city's traffic has been getting worse every year. But don't worry. I have some juicy details about my operation that will make the traffic jam worth it.

Saru: Unfortunately, it appears that in a few years, we will all be expert multitaskers, just like the Bangaloreans. Even in the midst of traffic chaos, they have mastered the art of remaining productive. Ufff… Now spill the beans. What's cooking under your operation?

Rishi: Nah, you go first.

Saru: Nope. You go first.

Rishi: Okay, after we talked and decided, I went to the restaurant and enlisted the help of a restaurant insider to check the surveillance footage, but there was no evidence of such an incident after reviewing the footage. I asked more questions about that evening, but nobody could offer any evidence or mention of such an incident happening.

Saru: If an incident had occurred, you would have gathered the information.

Rishi: Saru, What exactly are you saying?

Saru: Yes, Rishi, it appears from the information you have gathered that the incident you were looking into did not take place. I can add something to make it distinctive.

Rishi: What is it, Saru?

Saru: Sindhu became as pale as a sheet when I suggested calling the police and asking for their help. She tried to convince me that doing so would have unimaginable repercussions and then immediately sent a text message to someone while backing away from me. So it is now obvious and transparent that Sindhu made up the story she told us about the incident in order to deceive us; it was a fabrication that didn't actually take place.

Rishi: Yeah, it all makes sense, as I started connecting all the dots right from the beginning.

Saru: Despite not being able to see the entire house, I was able to cover her bedroom more thoroughly than other areas.

Saru instructed Rishi to "look at these pictures" while displaying the mobile gallery. As Rishi scrolled through the photos, he asked Saru, "Who is he?" And I see him in most of her pictures. He cannot be her brother because she is an only child and has no siblings.

Saru: He might be her cousin, Sonu, and they are close.

Rishi: Okay, it would be better for us to check if there is a recent picture of him. Anyway, how did you gather this much information?

Saru: That's not a lot.

Rishi: Okay, I have a sense of familiarity with his face, even though I am unable to recall the time and place where I may have seen him before.

Saru: That's interesting. Even if we can't remember the specifics, sometimes a familiar face brings back memories of previous encounters. Perhaps with more context or information, you will be able to pinpoint where you have seen him before, with the hope that this will lead us to the next level of understanding the situation.

Rishi: Let my mind work on this; I'm sure to solve it eventually. Anything else to say?

Saru: Oh boy, it looks like your brain is working harder than a hamster on a wheel! Don't worry, Rishi; you'll crack that soon enough.

Rishi: Oh, Saru. Don't be too jealous of my hamster-like brain power! If you are interested, I can give you some tips on how to keep up with my intellectual prowess.

Saru: Tell me the truth; you must have been drinking from the fountain of intellectual superiority!

Rishi: Haha, well, let's give our bodies and minds some time to rest so we can return with renewed vigor. By the way, I forgot to mention that I met Sanjay on the way. He was sorry for not spending time with us in the past couple of days and also for denying our invitation that night.

Saru said, "Oh," with a face of no interest in hearing about his details.

Rishi: Hey, Saru, Sanjay exclaimed that he called you and didn't hear back from you.

Saru: He did call me when I realized it was night, but I didn't bother to answer because it was late and I was feeling sleepy. However, I plan on returning his call at a later time.

Rishi: Okay, Saru. However, despite the fact that you resemble a pug exactly with your wrinkled forehead and squished nose and look endearingly cute and comical, what's the reason?

Saru: I can't help but feel a sense of worry and concern when I think about Sanjay's sudden disappearance and refusal to spend time with us. The events of that fateful night, when you opened up about the difficult experiences you've faced, still weigh heavily on my heart, and I wonder why all of a sudden everything was going wrong.

Rishi: Yes, as you said, this is all part of our testing phase. The night will pass, and we anticipate a sunny morning. So just be cheerful.

Saru's head bobbed up and down like a nodding toy as they chatted and strolled towards Rishi's room. When they finally arrived, Saru's eyes bulged with fury at the chaotic state of the room. Unable to contain her frustration, she let out a loud exclamation, demanding to know, "What on earth have you done to the room?"

Rishi: Uffo, Saru! I know the room is a bit of a mess right now.

Saru: Hey, a bit of a mess? It looks like a tornado hit a store and left a trail of debris in its wake. Why can't you keep things organized around you? Or at least let the helper do it.

Rishi: Please don't let the words come from you like a whistling pressure cooker. But before you turn into a temperamental pug, just hear me out. I was planning on cleaning up after coming home from the restaurant, but I had to visit you and give you the details.

Saru struggled to keep her cool as she surveyed the chaotic state of the room. The situation would only get worse if she gave into her escalating rage, much like a forest fire. Recognizing the importance of keeping the situation under control, she considered pushing Rishi to clean up the mess.

Rishi: Hey, Saru, cheer up. Ok, alright then, it's time to put on my cleaning hat and get this room shining like a polished masterpiece! I will be dusting, polishing, and organizing like a trained professional from urban cleaning home services, and I bet you doubt my cleaning abilities.

Saru took a deep breath, let a tiny smile spread across her face, and stated, Rishi, I have to admit, I was shocked at the condition of the room, but I am glad you are in charge of cleaning it.

Rishi: I just stopped a volcanic eruption, huh? and took her hand into his. How about each of us grabbing a broom? We'll make it worth your while with some momos from Beach Road later.

Saru: What if I propose a tasty addition, some chicken soup from the same place, to make it more mouthwatering?

Rishi: Haha, as you say, boss lady, you take care of this side of the room, and that side is mine.

As Rishi diligently dusted the cluttered bookshelves, Saru frantically cleaned up the mess he had made on the other side of the room. She was gathering the strewn clothing from the sofa when she noticed a mysterious gift box tucked away in the midst of the disarray. As soon as she realized what it was, she tried to force open the box's lid. When it did, she discovered a collection of photographs, just as Rishi had mentioned. She exhaled in shock as she began to notice them one by one. She cried as tears flowed down her cheeks, and she cleared them, spreading them across her cheeks. As she sank to the ground, she held the box tightly.

Saru's voice trembled with a cry as she reacted, "I am here," when asked, "Hey Saru, I don't see you. Where are you?"

Rishi followed her voice, and he noticed her seated on the ground near the opposite end of the bed; she was in a kneeling position with her head lowered in a sunken manner. He kneeled down in front of her and asked her, "Are you alright?"

Saru's face dropped as she handed the photos to him, her expression filled with regret. Rishi sighed, acknowledging his own mistake.

Rishi: Ugh, my bad. I should have kept these photos somewhere in the cupboard or discarded them. I can understand how you must be feeling about them, and that is precisely why I chose to keep them to myself and prevent you from seeing them.

Rishi's face lifted slightly as Saru comforted him, "Hmm, don't blame yourself." However, Saru's attention was drawn to the gift box wrapper as she let out an exclamation of pain and sadness, saying, "Oh my god, Rishi, you should see this."

Rishi: What came down?

Saru: Just a moment; pass me my mobile.

As Rishi gave the mobile to Saru, she went through the photos she had taken at Sindhu's place on her mobile. She stopped scrolling when she came across a picture of a gift wrapper and showed it to Rishi.

Rishi: It's the same. How could it be possible on Earth?

Saru: Even the design and texture of the paper are the same, and I felt it with my own fingers. What do we do now? Rishi.

Rishi: While there is a possibility that Sindhu may have played a role in the situation, it's important not to draw any definitive conclusions based on weak evidence like a gift wrapper. We need more convincing evidence before making a judgment or taking any action so that we can determine the extent of Sindhu's involvement.

Saru: Hell yeah. But it's certain she's part of it.

The ringtone played, as Saru put it, and they paused their conversation as their mobile device received an incoming call. Rishi turned the mobile to check the display and exclaimed, "Look, who decided to grace us with their call? It's Sanjay!" But it seemed that Saru wasn't in the mood for a talk with him at that moment. Rishi reassured her, saying that she could reach out to Sanjay later when they were in the mood for some scintillating conversation. Saru's phone buzzed with a message tone; it seemed like Sanjay dropped her a message, said Rishi.

Rishi: Giggled. Saru, I am reading out the message for you, "I'm having a craving for some good company and tasty food; can I tempt you into joining me for a meal?"

Saru: Hmm, what are you typing for him? I bet you don't type something that puts me in trouble and send him a message denying his polite invitation to dinner.

Rishi: Saru, I suggest you take Sanjay up on his offer and enjoy a scrumptious meal. Who knows, it might even be worth it just to see the look on Sanjay's face when you surprise him with a yes!

Saru: Hey Rishi, enough of teasing me! You have been telling me about eating, so I am not going to let those chicken-stuffed momos and piping hot soup slip through my fingers! And while we were on the subject, have you taken a look at my side of the room? It's practically sparkling clean, while your side still looks like a tornado swept through it!

Rishi: Why are you denying having dinner with a beguiling charmer? Anyway, it's your call, and Saru, I am here like a beaver, doing my given job with discipline. I mean, sure, we were having a great chat, and as I gave my full participation and gave a hundred percent like a hardworking donkey, I still got scolded. You blame the phone calls and messages that put a full stop to my ongoing work.

Saru: Ugh… You and your animal examples, ugh... Where do you get these? How do you connect everything to wildlife?

Rishi: Haha, so you want to know where I get my animal examples from? Well, let me tell you, I have a secret zoo hidden in my brain. Yep, it had everything from A to Zebra! And let me tell you something: connecting everything to animals is like a real giraffe... I mean, it's a real stretch.

Saru: Euff... easy, and you are so good with pun-tastic examples of animals. Listen, here is the deal: You need to start hustling and get your side of the room in order, because once we're both done, we're going to satisfy my insatiable cravings for those momos and soup. Trust me, if we make it late, there won't be a single crumb of momos in the food truck.

Rishi: Okay, okay, Saru.

Sita rapped on the door, and Saru walked to open the door.

Sita: Sanjay Sir has come and is waiting in the hall, and I informed him about your presence along with Rishi Sir.

Saru responded, "Please let him know that we will meet him shortly." and she expressed gratitude to Sita as she exited the room. Observing Sita leaving the hallway, Saru asked Rishi about the purpose behind this unexpected and unannounced visit.

Rishi: Well, maybe he called you to inform you that he was coming.

As they sauntered towards the hall to meet Sanjay, Rishi and Saru made a curious and peculiar decision. Instead of following the well-trodden and usual path, which involved exiting through the main entrance of Rishi's home and reentering from the entrance of Saru's home, they opted for a forgotten shortcut, shrouded in secrecy and known only to the family members.

The shortcut had been sealed off and abandoned for many years. When the two ancestral houses underwent extensive renovations, the outcome turned into ultra posh modern houses. But Saru and Rishi insisted on preserving its essence, and they shared nostalgia. The remodeling efforts had been compromised, allowing the shortcut to remain closely intertwined with the original structure. The rough, unplastered walls bore witness to the passing of time, adorned with faded paintings and drawings, especially the color pencil and crayon scribblings of Rishi and Saru as kids, which had stood the test of time.

As a decorative door, its exterior blended with the surroundings and was positioned adjacent to Rishi's room. Rishi exerted a gentle push, causing the door to swing open soundlessly, revealing the dark pathway.

Before them stretched a lengthy and not very narrow pathway. The absence of natural sunlight rendered the passage dim, but Saru located a series of lights positioned strategically along both sides of the walls. With a simple flick of a switch, the corridor became bright and warm. The illumination revealed the details on the wall. They both teased each other and reached the other side of the passageway, which was located beside Saru's room. They both walked to the hallway, where they saw Sanjay sitting on the sofa and having been served some tea and fritters.

Sanjay: Hey, hi guys!

Rishi: Hi Sanjay. Finally, I could see you today, even though you are in the same city and nearby. You are like a platypus because you are mysterious all the time.

Saru: Hey Sanjay. Omg, Rishi! Please spare us the animal kingdom. We had an agreement, remember? No more furry friends, in our words. The animal quota has officially been exceeded for the day.

Rishi: Okay, Saru, I hear you loud and clear, putting a pull stop, but it's hard to resist the temptation of using animal-language.

Laughter burst from three of them, filling the air with a sense of joy and happiness.

Sanjay: By the way, I was confused with the entry of you both coming from inside, as you both were in another home. How did you guys manage to slip past my watchful gaze while I remained glued to this sofa?

Saru: Oh, dear observer, you caught us. You see, me and Rishi possess mystical powers of invisibility. Just kidding, Sanjay, that we have a connecting way between the houses.

Sanjay: Interesting!

Rishi noticed Sanjay was having difficulty holding the coffee cup and asked, "Why that bandage on my fingers?"

Looking at his fingers, Sanjay said, "Oh, this is nothing, just a paper cut."

"A paper cut?" said Rishi and Saru.

Sanjay: Yeah, the cut is small but surprisingly painful because the paper's edge is sharp and thin.

Saru: Ah, you should cast aside the pernicious papers that threaten to slice and dice our fingers and instead spend some time in enjoyment. We are planning to have some yummy food near Beach Road. Would you care to join us?

Sanjay: Ha, sure. Thank you for your advice. Well, someone actually denied my request for good food and quality time. Anyway, I don't mind. Then you just share the location, and I will join you guys there.

Saru understood the counter and chose to remain silent. Rishi invited Sanjay and insisted that they go together, but Sanjay insisted and convinced him that he had an urgent meeting since the meeting was prefixed with the client virtually, and asked Rishi to share the location. Sanjay waved goodbye and quickly left the premises.

Rishi: Saru, What can be said about Sanju's swift appearance and disappearance, which resemble fireflies?

Saru: Yeah, Rishi, tapping her index finger on her lips. Something doesn't feel right about him when I think about his unique trait.

Exiting the house, they both shrugged off their previous discussion. Rishi squinted his eyes as he said, "Let it be about Sanjay; we have so much on us to solve and delicious hot momos to eat." They both waited outside, leaving the house behind. As the driver parked the vehicle in front of them, both of them slid into the back seats. Rishi directed the driver to take them to the destination, but upon seeing Raju, Saru's joy on her face faded.

Rishi gave the driver instructions to park the car close to the food court area as they approached the beach area. Rishi and Saru stepped out of the car.

stomachs fully full, sniffing the aroma of momos reaching their noses, which urged them to eat as quickly as possible.

Saru eagerly took a few more steps towards the food truck and placed an order of momos and soup. She turned completely and darted her eyes for Rishi, but she saw Sanjay walking towards her with a broad smile.

Sanjay: Hey Saru.

Saru: Hey Sanjay, Wah, right on time.

Sanjay: So didn't you want to reply to my call and deny my invitation to go out?

Saru: Hey, the other day it was late when you called me, and about today's call, that's when I and Rishi were elbow-deep in cleaning his room, and while I was about to make a call, I was elated that you made a physical call.

Sanjay: Saru, I realize that you are upset with me for not showing up when I was invited, and I am sorry for my actions.

Saru: Hey, Sanjay, chill. We are friends, and there is no need for apologies between us.

Sanjay: Yes, cool.

Saru: Of course. Where is this Rishi, and where has he gone? Why is it taking him so long to come here? Let me go around and search for him.

Sanjay: Hey, you stay here, and I will go and check for Rishi.

Saru: Nah, it takes time for the man to serve us.

I've tried calling Rishi, but he hasn't shown up, so I'll join you.

As Sanjay and Saru walked, she kept attempting to call his phone as they talked. They arrived at the location where Rishi and she had exited the car. She didn't find him there, and they both agreed to walk forward. After a while, they took a brisk walk in the right direction, and they found Rishi.

Saru couldn't help but show her impatience as she watched Rishi take longer than expected to arrive and questioned his tardiness. Sindhu, who had been hiding behind Rishi, startled Saru when she materialized in front of her.

Sindhu: Surprise! Surprise!

Saru: Hey, Sindhu, I'm certainly surprised to see you here. How did you get here?

Saru spoke with a disliked feeling but showcased a loving emotion. She hated to think about wasting time here talking about irrelevant matters, and she cherished the thought of savoring the long-awaited delicious food. She found it difficult to stand and act, as she enjoyed Sindhu's blabbering.

Sindhu: While driving to my aunt's house, which is located near a beach road, I happened to spot your car, so I called Rishi for a short and sweet meeting.

Saru: Ah, that sounds cute and romantic, giving Rishi a cheesy look. Why don't you join us to eat?

Sindhu: No, thank you; I am full.

Realizing the mistake, Rishi quickly corrected himself, introducing Sanjay to Sindhu as his friend. Sindhu and Sanjay exchanged pleasantries and engaged in a formal introduction.

After the brief interaction, Sindhu announced her looming departure, saying goodbye to all. She expressed her appreciation for the meeting and addressed Sanjay specifically, saying, "It was a pleasure meeting you."

Rishi and Saru remained silent as the three of them walked to the food venue, where a food truck man served them hot momos and soup. In a flash, they all gulped down the food.

Sanjay: Thank you for the tasty treat. I would adore to stay and spend more time with you both, but I have calls for a number of one-on-one meetings due to my decision to work from home for a few days and a ton of unfinished business that needs to be attended to. I'll be back in full swing soon. Goodnight guys.

Saru: Good night, Sanjay. Rishi, let's take a long walk. I am not sleepy, and it's been a while since we both went to the beach.

Rishi: Okay, wait a minute; let me inform the driver to get the car keys so we can go near the shore.

Saru: Hmm, yeah.

In a while, Raju popped up and handed the car key to Rishi, and Raju mentioned that it was getting late and he wanted to go home. Rishi responded, Okay,

Saru and Rishi were prancing with delight as they made their way towards the shore, and on the side, Saru asked Rishi to get popsicles for her and him.

"Grape or orange?" Rishi inquired.

Saru: Hmm, let's have one of each. Hehe.

Rishi: You won't change, Saru.

Rishi and Saru stride down playfully, relishing their popsicles, and eventually they choose a spot to sit.

Rishi: Sindhu's short meeting doesn't sound accidental. I was off to see her.

Saru: I understand Rishi; how could she recognize our cars? She must have done her homework, but this is a recent purchase, and moreover, you weren't driving the car.

Rishi: Sindhu must have had the eyes of a hawk.

Saru: Ugh, I am serious about it. Did you observe her while she was introducing herself to Sanjay?

Rishi: No, I don't like to be beside her, and you were talking about observing her. Anyway, what to do with it, Saru?

Saru: For a flash, I had a feeling that they were acquainted with each other, and in fact, I even had my eyes on Sanjay too, and he said bye as he had to go with Sindhu.

Rishi: What…? You might be overthinking Saru. Just to clarify, Sindhu and Sanjay definitely weren't in the same school. I told you we worked together on a project, and his city is Bangalore. Anyway, anyone can be friends with anyone from any corner of the globe. To clear up the confusion, have you considered checking their social media accounts? It could help in clearing the latest mental blocks that you are experiencing.

Saru: Hmm, I have done it; no use.

Rishi: You are excessively quick, Saru. After a long time basking in the comforting breeze's coolness, I am feeling at ease.

Saru: Yeah, serenity. Speaking of which, how long is Sanjay planning to stay here, and have you got extra keys for our guest house?

Rishi: Sanjay mentioned that he had some work in the city and was planning to extend his stay in the guest house, and I agreed to that, but I am unsure about the extra keys to the guest house, and I need to confirm with the manager. By the way, what is there to do with the extra keys?

Saru: Huh. You just clear it with the manager and get me the keys by tomorrow morning.

Rishi: Don't tell me that you are going to the guest house without Sanjay's concern.

Saru: You guessed it right, and promise me not to lecture me on being a good human with theories and speeches.

Rishi: Saru.... But why?

Saru: Allow me to delve into the details and thoroughly address my doubt, ensuring no clue is left unattended. I have a doubt, and I want to clear it.

Rishi: You made it sound simple, but it's not that simple to go and check the guest house when he is not inside the home.

Saru: Uffo, I will take care of it.

Rishi: If you'd like, after you've had your fill and are satisfied, let's go home so we don't get caught and interrogated for skipping dinner by someone inside the house.

Saru: Yeah, let's go.

Saru offered her left arm to Rishi for support to pull her along, and as he did, both of them seemed to have brushed the sand off the backs of their clothes. After walking to the car, Rishi opened the door of the driver's seat and was immediately hit with a strong smell of champak, and he forcibly pushed the door.

Saru: It's a new baby; why did you close with so much strength? Can't you be gentle?

Without saying a word, Rishi paved the way for Saru to open the door by remarking, "Yeah, why don't you just demonstrate to me?" Accepting the invitation, Saru stepped forward with confidence to open the door. However, the potent aroma of champak blocked her nostrils, resulting in a series of sneezes before she firmly shut the door.

Rishi teased Saru with a playful chuckle, saying, "Haha, hey, Saru, treat it gently; it's a new baby, you know."

Saru sighed in frustration. "Oh no, not again. I can't take it any longer," She said. The fragrance of champak triggered memories of their visit to the fishing harbor road with their cousins, where they encountered the pungent odor of deceased and dried varieties of sea creatures.

You remember it vividly, Saru continued, recalling the past. "As we ventured deeper into that road, you vomited with each step." She spoke with a mix of amusement and reproach.

Ceasing her laughter, Rishi responded, "Stop laughing, Saru. You know you were the one filming it and creating an embarrassing reel. Our cousins and friends made it go viral, and even our parents enjoyed it, leaving comments."

Saru replied, "Who can possibly forget that, Rishi?"

Rishi proceeded to open the car doors and pull out the mouth masks from the seatback pockets. He promptly put one on for himself and handed another to Saru. Both of them took a few steps away from the car to ensure they wouldn't inhale the potent scent of champak.

Rishi: Saru, when we came here, I sprayed a customized air freshener, which was subtle and pleasant. How does this strong aroma get trapped inside the car? What would happen to cause this blast of rancid odor?

Saru: Ugh, I know who would have turned the pleasant aroma into a source of pungency. I wish he was here, in front of me.

Rishi: Calm down. Who is that?

Saru: The driver, Raju.

Rishi: What? You mean the newly appointed driver?

Saru: Ugh, can you believe the tomfoolery I had to weather this morning? That blockhead, who apparently has no sense of social behavior, made me feel extremely uncomfortable with his creepy watches while I was on my way home. And if that isn't enough, I saw him in the kitchen assisting Sita, who filled the kitchen with strong smells. Despite being told that perfumes are sprayed and that baths are not recommended, he went ahead and did it by transforming a brand new car into a source of strong smells. Honestly, the depths of his stupidity are too deep to understand.

Rishi: Oh, so much has happened. Tomorrow, when he comes, I will talk to him.

Saru: Yeah, but what now? How will we be going home now?

Rishi: It's too late to send you in a cab; if you make a call to any driver, our parents will know about food truck dinners, and in particular, my mom puts both of us on a special, customized diet.

Saru: Ugh, what to do then?

Rishi: As we were wearing masks and I had opened the car doors for a while, the smell might have dissipated into the air to some extent. Close your nose with your hands; I will drive home in a jiff.

Saru acclimated herself to the disappointing circumstances, affirming, "Ah, this will work out and represents a better plan for now."

Saru and Rishi made their way home in the car, although they were not enthusiastic about it. Upon reaching home, Rishi advised Saru to use the stairs instead of the elevator, after which she said goodnight and departed.

Rishi then parked the car in its designated space before heading to his room. As he opened the door to this room, he detected a strong champak scent, which he assumed had been absorbed by his clothes from the car. Totally ignoring it, he went to bed after freshening up.

When Rishi awoke the next morning, his phone was flooded with messages and missed calls from Saru. When he opened the chat box, his attention was drawn to Saru's urgent text, "Come to my room." Reading through the messages and taking note of the numerous unanswered calls, he quickly understood the gravity of the situation.

Determined to address the matter instantly, Rishi got ready and set off to meet Saru.

The door to Saru's room was wide open, and upon entering the room, he closed it and walked in without announcing or alerting Saru to his presence. However, to Rishi's surprise, Saru was nowhere to be found in the room. He called her name, and the room remained silent, devoid of her response.

Rishi took a moment to observe the room's ambiance, which appeared new and unique to him. A soft candlelight flickered. He was overcome with drowsiness and tiredness and sought refuge in the inviting expanse of the bed. He wrapped himself in the sheets, sought comfort, and slowly drifted off.

After a few minutes, Saru emerged from the restroom, her body adorned with a towel that exuded a captivating radiance with its silky, shiny texture. Catching sight of the disarrayed sheets strewn across the bed, she approached with the intention of tidying them up. However, her gaze fell upon Rishi lying on the bed, and she let out a startled shout, which echoed through the room.

Jolted by her shout. Rishi swiftly joined her in a mixture of alarm and curiosity, their voices intertwining in a moment of shared astonishment.

Saru: What exactly are you doing here? And why are you shouting?

Without even a momentary averting of his eyes, Rishi was enraptured by the beauty of the skin that was visible beneath the fabric, which seemed more supple, silky, and shiny. It was as though he were seeing something exquisite and delightful with his eyes. The scent of a fragrant bouquet of roses permeated the air, adding to the enchanting atmosphere.

Saru: Hey, why are you looking at me as if you were seeing me for the first time?

Rishi: Yeah, this is the first time like this.

Saru: What? Nuthead, speak properly. I have to tell you so much. Why are you not speaking properly? Did I wake you up?

Rishi: giggled, In the tender depths, you stirred all the senses.

As the realization dawned upon Saru that Rishi had caught a glimpse of her in minimal clothing, a blush crept across her buccal pads, causing her to hasten her step towards the wardrobe.

With a sense of urgency, she selected the garments she intended to put on, swiftly closing the closet doors behind her. Sensing a mix of embarrassment and shyness, she called out to Rishi, urging him to avert his gaze and keep his eyes closed until she had finished changing.

Saru approached Rishi with newly gained assurance, and her shyness was still visible in the slight flush on her cheeks. As they exchanged glances, a subtle tension permeated the space between them. As they sat close together, the lub and dub sounds of their hearts beating in sync echoed in the air like a sweet melody.

Rishi decided to break the silence and quoted, "Saru, what was the urgency with which you left so many messages and missed calls?" Saru was still floating in the thoughts of the electrifying feeling that happened to her for the first time and wholly ignored the words of Rishi.

Rishi observed that she wasn't listening to him, and he walked to her and said, "If you were flying in your dreamland, would you do the landing and please pay attention to my words?" and placed a hand on her left shoulder.

Saru quickly refocused her attention on Rishi's words by fluttering her eyelids open and shut. "Yes, I am listening closely; what is it that you want to say?"

Rishi: Look, who is saying this? You called me here!

Saru: Yeah, yeah, last night when I entered the room, I felt the scent of champak, which means the driver would have entered my room.

Rishi: Oh, I even experienced the same thing, but I thought it might be coming from the clothes absorbed while traveling in the car.

Saru: I believe he definitely entered our rooms; how dare he?

Rishi: But why would he do that?

Saru: Omg, he could be the one who fixed the cameras in our rooms.

Rishi: Oh God, there are chances, but how would we confirm them? Saru

Saru: When did he join as a driver? Do you have any ideas? Let's check his background and monitor him closely; we could find a way to catch the main person.

Rishi: Yeah, Just two days before we throw your birthday party, that sounds good. Ok, then, let's have some breakfast, and I will start the job.

Rishi and Saru had breakfast and simultaneously discussed and planned things to do in the day.

Sanjay's mobile screen lit up, revealing a message that spoke of their reunion after a span of three days. Sanjay's heart warmed as he read the words because they exuded a sense of happiness and made a call to her.

Sanjay: Hello, you shouldn't have come there to see me; could you just imagine the damage if they understood that we were together? Luckily, we just missed, or else we would have been caught because of you.

Sindhu: Hey Sonu, Why would we? Anyway, don't be furious now; I just came to see my Sonu, and I left too soon.

Sanjay: Oh, Sindhu, please. We planned to meet tonight; why did you come yesterday?

Sindhu: Ugh, we didn't get caught, and I can't wait too long to see.

Sanjay: By the way, how did you come to know where I was?

Sindhu: Oh, I called Raju, and he gave me the information.

Sanjay: Ugh, this idiot, who can't keep things to himself; I instructed him many times not to pass on the information, and it would be unwise to underestimate arrogant ignoramuses, especially Saru; if you had lingered for another couple of minutes and made prolonged eye contact, she may have become suspicious.

Sindhu: Huh, enough, Sanjay, now tell me at what time I can expect you? And what do you like to eat for dinner?

Sanjay: Regarding time, I can't mention it now because you will be on the job of reminding me about dinner and about what to eat, whichever tasty food goes for me.

Sindhu: Haha, ok. Then see you soon.

Rishi and Saru finished breakfast and took the shortcut to reach Rishi's room. As they both stepped onto the path, the strong scent of champak greeted their senses, and they exchanged a confident glance before proceeding forward.

Saru said that her anticipation had proven correct regarding the driver. He found access to a shortcut and managed to fix the cameras in our rooms. Rubbing her nose against her left hand's sleeves, she found the smell to be irritating to her nostrils.

As they entered the room, Saru expressed her explosion of anger and sense of betrayal, questioning how the person working under them could have turned against them. Noticing Saru's distress, he reached out to a tissue holder, retrieved a tissue, and handed it to her.

Observing Saru's reaction, Rishi saw her place the tissue against her nose, inhaling deeply and exhaling, repeating the process several times to clear her nasal passages. Curious about their next course of action.

Saru: So, what do we do now?

Rishi: Tonight, the appointed person will be following Raju closely and providing us with the required information about his activities and whereabouts. In the meantime, I thought it would be a great opportunity to invite Sindhu for dinner, as we discussed in the morning. I believe sharing a meal might give us the chance to get to know her up close and have her phone as we planned.

Saru: Perfect; I was also thinking the same, and dinner would be perfect, and I have a plan for the next. You just make sure of her presence at dinner.

After their discussion of the plan for the rest of the day, Rishi expeditiously took the initiative to put the plan into action. He dedicated his time to exquisitely refining it, ensuring everything was in order. Soon enough, he reached Sindhu through a phone call and extended an invitation for dinner at his place.

Sindhu, without speaking much, responded with a resounding and happy yes. Her eagerness to accept the invitation was palpable, and as soon as she ended the call with Rishi, she immediately dialed Sanjay's number.

Sindhu: Hello, Sanjay.

Sanjay: Yes, Sindhu, I will join you for dinner tonight. I am currently at work, and as I informed you earlier, I got a meeting with budding startups for the launch of our new product in cosmetics. So, please understand if I can't be disturbed right now. I have to attend, and I am keeping the phone.

Sindhu: Oh, please. Sanjay. I am clearly aware of your chock-full schedule; why don't you listen first? Rishi invited me to dinner at his place; did you get any invites from them?

Sanjay: Hmm, no. What would be the reason? Do you think they have any doubts about us?

Sindhu: Uff, I think it's just a casual invitation.

Sanjay: Okay, you go for dinner; after that, I will meet you.

Sindhu: No, I would love to spend time with you rather than go to his place for dinner. What if I call and tell him that I am sick and ask him to postpone the plans? We can both have a good time.

Sanjay: You are not doing anything such; Rishi invited you for the first time; don't ruminate much about it, and he is getting on our track slowly. Just be mindful of your surroundings when you are there for dinner. We need him to trust you more, and this is an opportunity not to be wasted.

Sindhu: Okay, but you promised to meet me after dinner.

Sanjay: I will come home, and now you get ready for dinner, and don't forget to spice him up.

Sindhu: Uff, what are you making me do, Sonu?

Sanjay: Sindhu, this shit is no fun to me; did you forget what Rishi and Saraswati did to both of us, especially me? I am all alone in this world because of both of them.

Sindhu: Sanju, please don't say that; I am there for you.

Sanjay: Hmm, sorry for my earlier words. I shouldn't have spoken that way to you. Just at once, everything came flooding back into my mind, overwhelming me with a wave of agonizing feelings and memories. Everything flashed in front of me.

Sindhu: I totally understand. Now cheer up, and I will be waiting to see you tonight.

Sanjay: Yes, my love, and I'm sorry once again.

Saru: Rishi, are you all set for the dinner blast?

Rishi: Ah, imagining having dinner with her in our house and thinking of the incident yet to happen makes me feel uneasy and weighs heavily on my mind, casting a somber and lethargic expression on my face.

Saru: Oh, Rishi, take it easy; I will be dining with you. You don't have to depict her as a vampire who is coming only to suck your blood.

Rishi: Haha, look who is trying hard to crack a joke against me.

Sindhu arrived at Rishi's home at precisely 7 of the clock and was greeted there by Rishi and Saru. They put on fake smiles and showered her with fake affection. Sindhu agreed and said she wanted to see the house when Saru asked if she would be interested in seeing it. The three of them entered the house, and as Sita closed the entrance door, a deafening silence descended on the surroundings. Rishi's and Saru's parents had left for a two-day weekend trip, leaving the house devoid of any other occupants except for Sita, the only staff member who stays inside the house because she was assigned a room.

Rishi turned to Sindhu, but his gaze fixed on a wall-mounted decorative piece in the center hall, completely avoiding eye contact, and he asked if she was hungry. Sindhu glanced at her wrist watch and replied that it was only seven past ten minutes, and there was no rush for her to eat. Saru then chimed in, offering Sindhu some juice or squash. Sindhu responded that she preferred juice and suggested citrus or pomegranate flavors. Saru nodded in understanding and quickly instructed Sita to procure a juice of Sindhu's preferred choice.

Sindhu inquired about the whereabouts of Rishi and Saru's parents, as their presence was noticeably absent. Rishi began to retort, but Saru cut him off. Just before you arrived, our parents had plans to attend a party, and they will be back in two or three hours. My mom and aunt prepared some dishes for you and asked me to apologize on their behalf for not being able to spend time with you at the moment.

Sindhu: Hey, Saru. It sounds like a kind and thoughtful gesture, and I am grateful for it. I am looking forward to enjoying the food they have prepared with love, and I don't feel the need for them to apologize.

Saru: Oh, how absolutely delightful of you, Sindhu. Ah, Sita is here. Sindhu, please have the juice.

Sita stood calmly; the glass rested upon an ornate silver tray, its surface gleaming with a mirror-like polish and adorned with a gracefully curved edge. As she extended the tray towards Sindhu, a warm smile beautified her face.

Gracefully accepting the glass of juice, Sindhu inquired, "And what about two?" Saru responded that she and Rishi just had a late evening snack a few minutes ago.

Sindhu: Ahh, Mosambi is very refreshing. Thank you, Sita.

Sita: smiled and responded, How do you know my name, Madam?

Saru and Rishi became alert and perked up like a pair of meerkats and directed their eyes and ears towards her to catch her retort. Sindhu quickly attempted to cover her tracks by saying, "I heard Saraswati calling you," while hiding her malicious smile.

Sita left the area without displaying any emotion. while Rishi and Saru were providing a house tour. Sindhu trailed along behind them, uninterested, sauntered, and preoccupied with thoughts of meeting Sanjay.

Sindhu's right ankle slipped off the carpet, and she said, "Ouch."

Saru: Hey, are you okay?

Sindhu: Yeah, I slipped, and I think my right ankle got twisted.

Offering her assistance, Saru extended her hand to Sindhu, saying, "Oh, let me help you, Sindhu." The gesture served as a supportive guide for Sindhu as she rose from the floor. As Sindhu regained her footing, she began to sway from side to side, her steps unsteady and unbalanced. Sindhu stood on her feet and started to sway to one side, then the other after taking a few steps, making it harder, and her ankle also appeared to be giving way as she struggled to walk with balance.

Saru turned back and looked into Rishi's eyes as an assurance that their plan was working.

Rishi: Sindhu, I think your ankle got hurt, and you were not able to make steps. If you don't mind, I can take you to the room.

Sindhu: Hmmm, I am fine, Rishi; I can manage.

Saru: Hey, Sindhu, let him help you.

Sindhu accepted the offered help without uttering a word of refusal, indicating her silent consent. Rishi carefully lifted Sindhu and carried her to the guest room, gently placing her on the bed. Concerned for her well-being, he instructed her to stretch her leg in an attempt to alleviate any discomfort.

Rishi observed Sindhu's ankle; he gently touched the affected area. Prompting Sindhu to express her pain upon his touch. Her voice suddenly escalated in volume, indicating an intense sensation when he pressed the forefoot portion of her ankle.

Understanding the severity of the situation, Rishi surmised that there might be a ligament tear or just a sprain.

Rishi: Saru, call the family doctor.

Sindhu: Hey, Rishi, I thank you for your concern, but I think I will be fine. It's most likely just a sprain. You see, I have had my fair share of broken bones since I was a young sports enthusiast. I have learned to handle breaks and cuts. All I need is a tropical spray and a painkiller.

Rishi: That's brave of you. Are you sure? If not, I can take you to the hospital and get an x-ray done.

Sindhu: No, no, Rishi.

Meanwhile, Saru exited the room quickly and reappeared moments later, carrying a painkiller, pain relief spray, and a glass of water. I'm so sorry guys, I ruined your mood, Sindhu said as she held up the medicine and water while looking directly into Saru and Rishi's eyes. It's only a sprain, and in a little while I'll be fine and back on my legs.

Rishi: Hey, don't be sorry. Sindhu, you will rest for some time and have dinner. I have a little work to finish.

As Rishi left the room, Saru turned off the bright lights, turned on the dim lights, and sat beside Sindhu, waiting for her to fall asleep. Saru moved her right hand forefinger from right to left and left to right in front of Sindhu's face, swapping the fingers to double-check whether she had truly fallen asleep. Saru clenched the phone tightly in her hand and dashed out of the room before Sindhu could awaken from the effects of the sedation.

Rishi was pacing like a restless tiger in front of the room, constantly glancing at his phone as if it held the secret to the most unsolved puzzles of the universe, eagerly waiting for the green light of success to shine through and Saru to emerge as a wonder woman with good news about the operation.

Rishi: What took you this much time? Is she made of lead? She weighs a ton.

Saru: Uffo, Rishi, that's bad; she denied it even though you took her into your arms, and now you are complaining about her weight.

Rishi: Okay, I am sorry for that. So, did you get it?

Saru: Before that, Rishi, I specifically told you to pull the carpet back slightly to make her fall, but it seems like you have gone too far. What if she actually has a ligament tear? We didn't intend to cause her any harm. Hopefully, our sedation and painkillers will keep her pain at bay for a while, giving us the opportunity to check her mobile.

Rishi: Saru, relax; no biggie; it's just a sprain. I pulled the carpet like a pro, making it seem like we didn't touch a thing. The reality is, she did the most epic slip and fall ever! painkillers and a pill to go to sleep, which will help ease her pain. Did you forget how she put me on sedation and I ended up like a sleeping koala?

Saru: Okay, okay, I totally get it. By the way, I was able to remove the phone from her tightly closed palm, but what should we do with the locked phone?

Rishi: Hand it over to me; I will have a look, Saru.

The mobile phone buzzed twice, its screen displaying the name "Sonu." Saru and Rishi exchanged glances, unsure whether to answer the call or not. Finally, Saru convinced Rishi that she would take the call. As she answered, a worried voice greeted her, saying, "Hey Sindhu, why haven't you been replying to the messages? I am so worried about you. Didn't I tell you to keep posting? Wait, why aren't you saying anything?"

Saru, introducing herself as Sindhu's friend, informed the caller, "Hello, I am Saraswathi. Sindhu has sprained her ankle and is currently sleeping. May I know your name?" Hearing Saru's name, Sanjay became tense and quickly responded, "I am her cousin; I will send the driver to your house." He abruptly ended the call.

Rishi: What did he say? Saru?

Saru: Rishi, I recognize this voice; I've heard it before, and he said he would be sending the driver home.

Rishi: Short time; it will take at least 45 minutes for the driver to arrive; we didn't even try unlocking her phone; what do we do now?

Saru: I suppose we don't need her phone; keep Sita here and let her know that if Sindhu's driver shows up, she should accompany Sindhu's departure and that I am going to the storeroom and will see you there.

Saru's words to Rishi reverberated with intrigue as a sense of secrecy and suspense hung in the air. Rishi called Sita, informed her, and plodded to the storeroom with heavy, unlimited knocking and thoughts of the reason for Saru's comments, contemplating refusing to unlock Sindhu's phone.

As Rishi entered the store room, which is expansive and extensive in size, as the kitchen and store room were common for both families and situated to the left of the kitchen, the store room was maintained meticulously and radiated cleanliness, unlike in many households where such spaces are neglected the most. On the right side of the room, organized with shelves stacked with loads of groceries and delightful treats On the left side of the store room, his attention was drawn as he found Saru standing nearby. The shelves held an antique trunk of metal with intricate designs and natural colors painted on all sides of the box of pembarthi, which contained the treasured belongings, carefully preserved in the form of beautiful albums, that captured memories from the very moment each family member came into this world, especially Rishi's and Saru's.

Rishi walked, taking the cat steps, and stood behind Saru as she searched for the school albums. She began picking one after the other because details like years were not mentioned on the cover page. Saru was engrossed in turning the pages when she felt a sudden touch on her shoulder.

Rishi: Saru, have you gone cuckoo? I hope you understand the urgency of our situation. We are under a time constraint to crack the mobile's password, and here you were flipping through the dusty old pages of the album. What is there to do with these?

Saru: Rishi, hold on a second. It's absolutely crucial that we locate the ninth-grade sports annual meet album. If you decide to join me on this quest, we might just be able to save our precious time.

With bated breath, Rishi stood alongside Saru as they delved into the realm of dusty old albums. As he flipped through the pages, a glimmer of hope sparked within Rishi's eyes. Rishi's keen eyes locked onto the elusive ninth-grade sports album. As Saru grabbed the album, she turned the pages with a fervor akin to a student frantically flipping through their notes before an important exam.

And there it was—a photograph that caught Saru's attention, freezing her in awe. With a mixture of excitement and curiosity, she held it up to Rishi, silently struggling to unravel the story behind the captivating image.

Saru: Rishi.... Look at this picture; the boy standing next to Sindhu is Sanjay.

Rishi: What are you saying, Saru? Why would Sanjay be in our school album?

Saru: No doubt, the person with whom I just spoke over the phone is Sanjay. Despite his attempt to alter his tone upon hearing my voice, I was able to recognize and catch him, leading me to the conclusion that he is none other than Sonu, our darling Sindhu's cousin.

Rishi: "What are you saying, Saru? I can hardly believe it myself. It's astonishing how you managed to track down the person, but how did you?"

Saru: Rishi, when we expressed our concern for Sindhu's sprained ankle, she casually mentioned her past experiences dealing with similar injuries. It instantly transported me to our school days, where Sindhu was one of the star athletes, consistently leading her team to victory. Remember the class-ninth sports meet? That's when I recall seeing Sanjay by Sindhu's side, cheering her on.

The outsider's presence made all the other girls jealous. Our captain requested that all the supporters join the photo session, and I'm glad that I took all the photos from the school other than a single groupie. But here is the kicker – the boy captured in the photos on Sindhu's wall and the one who cheered for her are the same. And that's not all! The gift wrapper paper I found at Sindhu's house and the one I saw at our guesthouse when I visited Sanjay match the wrapping cover of the gift sent to you. And my instincts were not wrong because, when we went to have momos, you got to introduce Sanjay to Sindhu, and I felt that they both knew each other.

Rishi: Oh my god, I won't leave that idiot, who is staying on our roof and stabbing us.

Saru: Yeah, Rishi, now let's go to Sindhu before she leaves our house, so we can know the reason for their intention to hurt us.

Rishi and Saru darted towards the dimly lit guest room, their hearts pounding with a sense of urgency. Saru's voice quivered with anxiety as she implored Rishi to make an immediate phone call to Sita.

Rishi dialed Sita's number and conveyed the message: Sindhu had to be restrained at all costs. Rishi couldn't help but ask a nagging question. "What if Sanjay suspects that we are onto him?"

Saru: I don't believe Sanjay knows yet, but we can't take any chances. We need to uncover the truth before he can make a move against us.

Rishi and Saru arrived in the room, feeling a mix of anticipation and exhaustion from their little sprint journey. They checked inside for Sindhu, and looking at her, they inhaled deeply to catch their breaths. The adrenaline was still coursing through their veins as they shared a fleeting instant, with Rishi gently holding Saru's hand and replying that having Sindhu here, under our control, will provide us with the answers we require.

They were driven by a desire for justice as well as a desperate need to find answers and explanations. Suddenly, Sita burst, delivering the startling news that Sindhu had regained consciousness, and she appeared visibly agitated and asked for her mobile.

This revelation set Rishi and Saru's plan into motion. Without hesitation, Saru instructed Sita to procure any available material, be it plastic or rope, to restrain Sindhu. Sita, grasping the magnitude of the situation, expeditiously gathered the requested items, not daring to question or reveal her surprise.

As they ventured into the room, Sindhu regained complete consciousness, and by looking at them, she put out a facade of innocence and illness and tried to wish for both of them. Rishi's anger boiled over, and he erupted in a fit of rage, accusing Sindhu of deceiving them.

Just as the tension reached its peak, Sita arrived with the required items. Working together rapidly, Rishi and Saru bound Sindhu's hands, effectively immobilizing her. Sindhu's voice echoed through the room, filled with a mix of fury and desperation, directing it at Rishi and Saru.

Saru: Shh, enough with fabricated and insincere pleas; it's become evident that your cries and emotions are fake and bogus.

Sindhu: Have you gone insane, Saru? What you are saying is completely nonsensical. Please refrain from making baseless accusations.

Rishi: Enough! Stop acting like a victim here. Right from the beginning, I knew that you were not a trustworthy person. All those stories you concocted were just ploys to make everything seem normal. You even involved Wamsi in your plan, pretending to get close to him. Wasn't it all part of your scheme to deceive everyone and make them believe you? You even used the alumni day to manipulate the situation and kidnapped me deliberately by injecting a drug into me. The most heinous part is that you didn't even go to the bar, but you pretended to have been harassed by some random guy there. You held my purse on purpose and invited me to the hotel to give it to you, but you made it look convincing for our parents to think that we are in love. With Raju's assistance, you installed cameras in our rooms. What have I done to deserve this betrayal?"

In the midst of the intense conversation, Sita interrupted, drawing everyone's attention, and informed them that the driver had arrived. Directing her sight towards Rishi, she questioned, "What information should I pass to him?" Hearing this, Sindhu's voice pierced through the commotion as she screamed, "Please, don't let him leave! I want to go home. Untie me, Rishi!" Rishi and Saru stood there, their faces filled with anguish, as they watched Sindhu's tantrums.

Saru: Oh, definitely Sindhu; we have no interest in keeping you here; we just want to know the reasons, and then you can leave; however, before you leave, you must tell your driver to return without raising any doubts with him.

Rishi: If you try to be smart, I will right away call the police, and we have all the evidence to screw you and your darling Sonu, alias Sanjay. I hope you are aware of the legal complexities surrounding the cases involving cheating and threats. I also hope you act in a way that protects your family's reputation. So, stay sober and inform the driver.

After contemplating for a moment, Sindhu looked at Rishi and comprehended that cooperation was the only viable option, as they seemed determined to extract all the necessary information from her. Understanding this, she nodded her head in agreement. Saru stepped forward, holding Sindhu's mobile phone in her right hand, and placed it in front of Sindhu, signaling her to unlock it. Using Siri, Sindhu contacted the driver and conveyed to him that she had decided to stay back and reach out when assistance was needed.

Rishi asked Sita to check whether the driver had departed or was still present. Upon receiving confirmation from Sita, Rishi told Sita to bring dinner for all three of them to the guest room. Sita hastily left the room to acquire the food for their dinner. Rishi and Saru drew their chairs closer to Sindhu, who sat on the bed with her hands bound. Sindhu appeared remorseful and guilty as she waited for their conversation.

Rishi: Good, I could see a little guilt on your face. Expose every detail.

Sindhu: Ahhh, stop blaming and projecting me as a criminal here; I just gave my support and joined Sanjay's hands to help him relieve excruciating pain and fulfill vengeance.

Saru: What has that to do with us? Give us a clear explanation without employing your canny and shrewd tactics and strategies. Just get straight to the point and communicate transparently.

Sindhu: Ha ha, what? How are you two expecting me to conduct myself with you two respectfully? Our lives were filled with darkness because of you both, and Sanjay's life in particular can no longer be made brighter. You both brutally murdered his parents and forced him to live alone, depriving him of all joy and love. It should be you two in jail, not me. Unfortunately, you both avoided the penalties and were able to live happily and freely with a mask of good and kind people.

Rishi and Saru found themselves completely overwhelmed by the shocking news they had just received. They were in a state of disbelief and struggled to comprehend the weight of the situation. As they both exchanged glances, their surprise was evident on their faces, and they couldn't fathom the accusations being made against them.

"What kind of blame game is this?" Rishi shouted, his voice filled with incredulity. We would never, not even as a joke, intentionally harm anyone. How could you possibly accuse us and think of us in such a way?" Saru, equally taken aback, added, "This is utterly insane, Sindhu. You are just spewing whatever comes to your mind without any basis."

As intense emotions and arguments filled the room, Saru's mobile rang, and it was Sita. Saru disconnected it, but Sita continued to call. Saru understood it could be an emergency and answered the call after disconnecting four times. As Saru heard Sita's trembling and anxious voice on the other end, a surge of panic compelled her to end the call and open the camera app on her mobile. Much to her surprise, the live feed displayed Sanjay rushing through the hallway, frantically checking each room. Following closely behind him, Sita could be seen shouting and desperately trying to stop him. Saru acted fleetly and alerted Rishi to close the door, ensuring a swift response to the unfolding situation.

Upon reaching the guest room, Sanjay's effort to push open the door proved futile, signaling that everyone must be confined inside. A sense of apprehension gripped him, and he realized that everyone must be inside that very room. Sita, trembling with fear, took deep breaths and managed to utter, "No one is here; it's an empty room."

Sarcastically, Sanjay, in response, let out a bitter laugh and proceeded to dial Sindhu's mobile. Despite it ringing, he couldn't detect any sound emanating from it. Undeterred, he decided to try Rishi's mobile, and to his relief, he heard the ringtone resonating from within the room. Sita remained silent, her expression giving nothing away. Frustrated and desperate, Sanjay continued to pound on the door, pushing it forcefully and shouting in a desperate attempt to gain entry.

Rishi relayed the message to Saru, urging her to hold onto Sindhu as he prepared to open the door for Sanjay. Rishi turned the doorknob and swung the door open, revealing Sanjay in a state of uncontrollable fury. His eyes were bloodshot, and his body seemed to radiate intense anger.

Without a moment's hesitation, Sanjay delivered a powerful push towards Rishi's stomach, aiming to cause him pain. In an instinctive response, Rishi swiftly retaliated by delivering a forceful punch to Sanjay's nose. Sanjay clutched his nose in agony, letting out a piercing scream as he felt the intense pain. He quickly inspected for any signs of bleeding, his gaze filled with determination. Resolute in his decision, he resolved to inflict the same level of pain on Rishi.

Witnessing the escalating violence, Saru became deeply concerned and feared that the fight would escalate even further. In an attempt to put a stop to the altercation. Saru cried out in a trembling voice, threatening to harm Sindhu with a knife, which was brought along with the rope she held in her hand. When Sindhu saw the gleaming blade in Saru's hands, she was so terrified that she let out a piercing scream.

Sanjay: Hey, don't hurt her; she's innocent; just leave her alone.

Saru: Sure, Sanjay, but only if you cooperate and do what I say.

Sanjay: Yes, yes. I will.

Saru: Good, then give your mobile to Rishi, and you walk directly into the room and sit in the chair assigned for you across from Sindhu. And if you attempt to outsmart or act cleverly, it will result in me causing harm to Sindhu by sliding the blade into her skin mercilessly.

Sanjay: No, no, I will do what you say. Please don't hurt her.

Following Saru's rigid words, Sanjay proceeded to walk as directed. Rishi tightly gripped Sanjay's hands from behind, exerting pain on his trapezius muscle, causing him pain, and he forcefully guided Sanjay into the room and thrust him onto a chair. Despite discomfort and pain, Sanjay maintained eye contact with Sindhu and felt sorry for putting her in such a traumatic situation. Saru poured water into a glass placed on the bedside table and handed it to Sanjay. Reluctantly, Sanjay accepted, with intense emotions boiling within him. Sita entered the room bearing an enormous tray that seemed far too heavy for her petite frame. However, she effortlessly carried it away and placed it on the table carefully. The aroma from the food spread throughout the room, enticing everyone's senses and causing stomachs to rumble in hunger.

Saru: Want to taste some food? Mr. Sanjay alias Sonu, but I think Moron suits you the best.

Sanjay: Damn, just leave us.

Saru: How could you falsely accuse Rishi and me of committing such a heinous crime, which we didn't commit? What was your motive for subjecting us to suffering through your actions? He is your good friend.

Sanjay: I find it completely unimaginable that I considered Rishi a good friend and could be responsible for the monstrous act of murdering my parents. Tragically, the lack of oxygen proved fatal before any rescue team could reach them, which caused their deaths.

Rishi: Sanjay, why would we both be the reason for the death of your parents?

Sindhu: Don't believe him; they must have executed everything under the influence of copious amounts of alcohol. Poor guy, how on earth could he possibly remember?

Rishi: I have never lost control due to alcohol or any other substance, and Saru has never touched it. How can you make such a false claim?

Saru: These allegations being made against us are completely false, and it appears that you both have some other motives behind these allegations.

Sanjay asked for his mobile phone to prove it, and Rishi told Sita to retrieve it. Sita positioned herself in front of Sanjay, who proceeded to unlock the screen. He then provided guidance to Sita on operating the device, advising her to locate the required album. As Rishi and Saru observed the photos, they were left speechless. Rishi and Saru could be seen standing in some of the photos, while others showed their car parked at the scene of the incident.

Sindhu: What happened to you both? Lost speech? You guys skillfully manipulated everything and escaped very smartly, evading any consequences.

Saru: Hey, Sindhu. For God's sake, will you shut your mouth? We didn't commit any murder, and we are not responsible for Sanjay's parents' deaths.

Rishi: What Saru is saying is absolutely right; trust me, Sanjay.

Sanjay: Then what have you got to say about these pictures? So you guys claim that you both were not in these pictures?

Rishi: It's we, but we weren't the reason for your parents' deaths. Two or three years ago, Saru, myself, and a few other friends went on a week-long trip to Lambasingi and stayed at a farmhouse. If you don't believe us, you can inform the police to investigate us.

Sanjay: Yes, our person from the farm witnessed you guys pushing our parents car into the valley as you lost control over the wheel due to overtaking alcohol, and definitely, you both are going to prison. Before that, I decided to give hell to you both.

Rishi and Saru were distressed about the allegations, and Sanjay and Sindhu were soaked in grief. Together, they made a joint decision to share the events of that fateful day. Taking charge of the situation, Rishi made a call to his uncle, ACP Raghu Ram, and informed him of the distressing news.

ACP: You and Saru should stay safe until I get home; I will be there right away.

Sita observed the troubled countenances and distressed visages and pondered what could happen in the next few hours when ACP comes here. She caringly urged everyone to eat. Regrettably, her kind gesture was met with disinterest, as was the weight of their bereavement, the loss of Sanjay's parents, and frustration over the accusations against Rishi and Saru. The grief and troubles seemed to have robbed them of their appetite. Determined Sita gently insisted again, and all of them, understanding the importance of sustenance in challenging times, managed to muster the strength to consume the humble bowls of soup and completely avoid the solids.

As the doorbell echoed, everyone was alerted, and Sita's anticipation grew. She briskly made her way to the entrance to welcome Mr. Raghu Ram. Being aware of his oncoming arrival, she swung open the door, greeted him with a respectful "Namaste Sir," and walked and gestured the way towards the guest room, maintaining silence.

Rishi and Saru's hearts swelled with relief as they witnessed the sight of Mr. Raghu Ram. Saru, overcome with emotion, dashed towards him, leaving Sindhu behind and bursting into tears, while Rishi approached him calmly and embraced him tightly. The presence of Mr. Raghu Ram left Sanjay and Sindhu baffled and anxious, their minds racing with the thought of potential consequences for their involvement in the blackmail and torment inflicted upon Rishi and Saru.

ACP: My dear Rishi and Saru, let me handle everything. We will take the necessary steps by filing a case against these two idiots for blackmailing and threatening you both. Their actions are unacceptable, and it is important that we stand up against their attitudes.

In a synchronized voice, Rishi and Saru firmly expressed their request to withhold any hasty actions against Sanjay and Sindhu. Their main intention was to demonstrate their innocence and debunk the unfounded allegations directed at them. Sanjay and Sindhu found themselves completely caught off guard by this unexpected stance, given the immense suffering and harm that Rishi and Saru had endured at the hands of their tormentors. The unexpected and surprising statement prompted a mixture of astonishment and confusion, leaving Sanjay and Sindhu uncertain about the appropriate course of action.

Meanwhile, Sita immersed herself in brewing a cup of flavorful spiced chai, knowing that Mr. Raghu Ram had an affinity for the beverage, regardless of the time it was served. With a warm gesture, she offered it to him, and he snuffed the chai aroma and accepted it with a bright smile on his face, as he was expecting the chai.

Mr. Raghu Ram enjoyed his cup of chai as he engaged in conversation with Sanjay and Sindhu. They both seemed a little cooperative. Mr. Raghu Ram took the opportunity to gather detailed information about the incident from them. He sternly warned both Sanjay and Sindhu against causing any harm to Rishi and Saru, stressing the ramifications they would face if they did. Mr. Raghu Ram made it mandatory that they visit the police station every day until the case was resolved, ensuring their involvement in the investigation process. Sanjay and Sindhu denied visiting the station daily as it could leave a mark on their reputation if their families or the media came to know. After much discussion and requests, Mr. Raghu Ram agreed with them on a few terms and conditions.

As nighttime approached, Mr. Raghu Ram announced that it was time for him and others to head home. However, he assured Rishi and Saru and told them not to share any news with their parents. Before leaving, he added that the following day they would all be traveling together to Lambasingi. After everyone dispersed, Rishi and Saru walked to the heart of the home. With relaxed expressions on their faces, they settled down on the comfortable sofa, allowing themselves to rest and decompress while engaging in lively chat and friendly banter.

Rishi: Saru, I can't tell you how relaxed I am feeling today after many days of worrisome living, and I must appreciate your astute brains for connecting the dots at the right time. Your abilities are remarkable, just like a border collie's.

Saru: Haha, wild life again, Rishi. Against the odds, the immense pain, and the countless tears we have shed, we have made significant progress in revealing the people who caused tumult in our lives, and there is still a long way to go to unravel every aspect of this perplexing mystery.

The relaxed atmosphere was further amplified when Sita joined them, taking control of the television and selecting a classic, timeless movie that never gets boring and can be enjoyed through repeated viewings. Just as they settled in, Saru's mobile phone suddenly began to ring, interrupting the entertaining calmness. Saru glanced at the caller ID and saw that it was Mrs.Sharmila. As Saru answered the call, Mrs.Sharmila informed her that all four would be running late and wouldn't be able to return home tonight. After exchanging some small talk, Saru ended the call.

With naughty smirks on their faces, everyone's eyes met, and a burst of laughter filled the room. Rishi's comment highlighted the success of their devised plan to engage parents at the party tonight. The cheerful aura pulsated with a sense of accomplishment as three of them luxuriated in the mischief they had conducted.

As the cinema carried on, Rishi and Saru found themselves dozing off in the same spot, their bodies intertwined in peaceful sleep like the tranquility of deep meditation. Meanwhile, Sita, lying on the carpet, relented and went to sleep as well.

The radiant morning sun poured its yellow and golden rays upon Sita's drowsy face, mischievously interrupting her tranquil sleep. Desiring a few more minutes of sleep, she adjusted slightly, evading the persistent beams. Unfortunately, the gentle chime of the doorbell jolted her awake with ruffled hair and bleary eyes, spurring her to rub her eyes and yawn widely. As she slowly made her way towards the door, the bell rang again, this time with more urgency. Sita quickened her pace, eager to see who was on the other side. She swung open the door and was baffled to see Raju at first light.

Driver: Good morning, Sita, Why did it take you so long to answer the door?

Sita: Good morning; I was sleeping; why did you show up too early in the morning?

Driver: I got a call from Mr. Srinivas sir asking them to pick them up from Mr. Naidu sir's Bheemili farm house around nine o'clock. I left early last night to go home, and I assumed there might be some work now.

Sita: Oh, well, it's not even six, and allegedly the world is desperately yearning for some work. It is fortunate that there is nothing. But don't you worry. As of now, nothing; if there are any updates, I will keep you informed as needed.

Goodbye for the time being as I plunge headfirst into this fascinating world of pots and pans.

Raju could not concentrate on Sita's blabbering, so he brushed it off and tried to peep into the house, his main goal being to find out why Sanjay and Sindhu had not returned his calls and messages. He was aware that Sindhu had been invited to this house for dinner the night before, and he was now concerned about them. But Sita, sensing something, rudely dashed the door in his face.

Rishi slowly awoke as the phone beeped, and as he opened his eyes, he noticed Saru sleeping with her head on his chest. He did not care to get up, and he thought how adorable she was with her hair flowing over her delicately contoured cheeks and narrowing down to a delicate jawline. The faint, enticing dark mole just below her nose and slightly above her lip on the right side of her face tempted him with the feeling of putting a tender kiss on it.

In the early morning sun, her face shone with a youthful and supple glow. With his right index finger, Rishi gently traced the lines of her face and felt the mole. Saru awoke as Rishi's breath caressed her skin, and as she realized he was so close to her, surprise danced across her face.

Saru: Rishi… You scared me.

Rishi: Shhh. Can't you sleep for some more time?

Saru: What? You sound different? What went into your head?

Rishi, in a hushed tone, whispered to himself, "Your beauty," hoping that Saru wouldn't catch his words. In an effort to rid himself of his attraction to Saru, he intended for it to act as a diversion by quickly adding, "Raghu Ram uncle sent a message, informing us that it was time to begin. So you please go and get ready as soon as possible."

In an hour, Rishi and Saru were served breakfast in the TV room as they wanted to have it while watching the remaining part of the movie, which was left as they dozed off. Sanjay and Sindhu walked into the hall with penitent and shameful looks. Raju saw Sanjay and Sindhu entering the house, and he rushed into the hall and shouted, Sanjay sir, neglecting his surroundings.

Sanjay gave Raju a scathing look for ignoring his surroundings and calling them names. Sindhu did not even bother to look at Raju.

Saru: Sanjay, please attend to your crony first; he came to our house in the first hour to learn about you, and you would have answered his calls. Raju, how unfortunate! Is that Sindhu? Or am I missing something?"

Sanjay: Raju, please kindly remain silent for a while. Saru and Rishi, there is a heartfelt apology I wish to extend to both of you. Yesterday, it became undeniably clear that the effects of our deeds went far beyond mere regret. My anger became all-consuming as a result of my intense grief over the loss of my parents, and I became a monster capable of inflicting unspeakable pain on the two of you.

Raju, who was listening intently to Sanjay's words, realized that the shell was cracked and fled the scene. Saru attempted to retort, but Rishi intervened by widening his eyes to catch her attention, and he signaled a halt. Rishi stated that if either of them had directly asked, we would have openly shared the information.

Sanjay and Sindhu bowed their heads in confession, but Sanjay still harbored the same level of resentment toward them. However, Rishi emphasized that it was now equally important for them to understand the cause of their parents' deaths. Sindhu moved forward and apologized for everything in response to Rishi's comments, but Sanjay remained standing.

Everyone eventually got in the car as the driver came over to tell them they had to leave and that Mr. Raghu Ram would be joining them there. Inside the car, the atmosphere excluded a sense of boredom, as if the management had imposed the compulsion and strict rule of attending additional chemistry classes on weekends. Except for Saru, who fell into a deep and restful sleep, unaffected by the tedious journey, the other passengers were all glued to their personal time-killing devices in an effort to break up the monotony. While the driver played his own collection of music at a subdued volume. After traveling for one hour, the vehicle was stopped, and Mr. Raghu Ram joined them.

Rishi: Hey, uncle, good morning!

ACP: Good morning, Rishi, oh! Look at Saru; she is lost in the depths of sleep. And you both, don't breathe a word about our visit to the farmhouse keeper that we are visiting; let's give them a surprise! Haha!

Rishi made a conscious decision to remain silent, while Sanjay and Sindhu expressed their agreement by nodding their heads. Mr. Raghu Ram instructed the driver to change the song playing in the vehicle and requested a recent hit from the movies.

As the journey progressed, the weather took a turn, becoming cloudy and bringing cool breezes. Saru, who had been asleep since the beginning of the journey, woke up and lowered the windows to fully immerse herself in the scenic beauty of nature. However, as it began to drizzle lightly, she closed the windows, adding to the fact that it wasn't straight as anyone had to take turns and more turns, and the driver took the vehicle at a slower pace. The journey continued for another two hours, enduring challenging stretches of rough, stony, and poorly maintained roads until they finally arrived at the village. The weather conditions throughout the journey remained unpredictable.

In the quaint village of Lambasingi, about thirty miles in the interior, on the wild coast, there was a charming and delightful farmhouse. The architecture exuded the essence of local culture with its rustic and traditional design, but the interior had been transformed to suit the modern and opulent taste of Sanjay's father. The farmhouse was tucked away in an idyllic setting, as depicted in the movies, and surrounded by vast plantations, primarily tea and coffee.

Frontside, a vegetable garden thrived, largely cultivating leafy and bulbous vegetables, along with a selection of perennials bordering the farmhouse and seasonal flowering plants adding a burst of color and fragrance to the surroundings, creating a habitat for an abundant variety of vivid and colored species of feathered friends. Many other charming farmhouses were scattered and given to tourists for money across the landscape.

Located a short distance away, about 100 meters from the farmhouse, stood a humble stack that elongated to Sankar Rao, a thin, dry man with glum eyes who managed the farmhouse from its inception, dedicating himself to its upkeep and growth. He earned his bread and butter solely from the resources of the farmhouse and the monetary tips given to him on the occasional visits to the farm by Sanjay's parents. Ever since his wife tripped over a stone in the field one day and fell full length on a venomous snake. When one is bitten in the chest, there is not much that can be done. He was left to care for their two children on his own. One is twenty three and the other is seventeen, though both are more or less dependent on their father.

In the infrequent occurrence of vehicles passing through the small mud way in front of the farmhouse, the distinct sound of the huge Toyota caught Mr. Shankar Rao's attention. He stopped cleaning in the kitchen right away and started to move in the direction of the noise. As he approached, his surprise intensified as he laid eyes on the packed car, revealing an unexpected and unannounced sight – Sanjay,

Sindhu, and several other members. The unexpectedness of their presence left Mr. Shankar Rao in a state of curiosity.

Mr. Shankar Rao: How are you, Sanjay? I didn't see you after the demise of your parents, and you didn't pay a single visit to the farmhouse later. I'm so happy to see you both.

Sanjay: I am good. How are you doing? I have been busy with work.

Mr. Sankar Rao: I am doing well. I understand and experience the pain that accompanies the loss of our loved ones, but I am happy that you both came.

Sanjay: Hmmm, I am sorry for your loss, and please take care of our guests.

One by one, they emerged from the vehicle, stepping out and stretching their bodies after the long journey. Without sharing the word, they instinctively moved toward the farmhouse. Mr. Sankar Rao kindly offered assistance to the members to carry the luggage inside, but each of them politely declined, shouldering their own backpacks and suitcases.

As they entered, they discovered the interior was just as enchanting as the exterior. The ground floor housed a cozy living room, adorned with comfortable and cushioning sofas and a fireplace that emanated a warm glow. A large wooden dining table stood before entering the open kitchen.

The farmhouse was constructed strategically and was spacious enough to accommodate many families. Mr. Raghu Ram and the driver settled into comfortable rooms on the ground floor, ensuring easy access for their needs. Meanwhile, Rishi and Saru were given rooms on the upper floor, where they could enjoy some privacy and a peaceful retreat.

Sanjay and Sindhu took the inside elevator to the second floor, which his parents had built based on Sanjay's preferences. Sanjay chose a spacious master bedroom on the upper floor because he enjoys the scenic views. This room featured a grand four poster bed draped in luxurious linens and large windows overlooking the sprawling countryside. There was an attached balcony where one could sit and enjoy the stunning sunsets and starry nights.

Everyone had gathered by lunchtime in the dining hall. Different varieties of dishes were placed on the table, mainly cooked with ingrown local vegetables, and All eyes searched for Mr. Raghu Ram. They waited, and after a while, he and the driver came from outside. After a handwash, they both joined them and had a simple and tasty lunch.

Mr. Shankar Rao: How is the food? My younger son, who is quite skilled in cooking, took charge of preparing every dish all by himself, and I am curious to know if everyone enjoyed the meals.

Sanjay: It's tasty; thank you, Hari.

Hari responded with a shy smile and looked at the rest of the group, eagerly anticipating their reactions. Rest all too praised and showered him with good compliments for his culinary talents. To his happiness, everyone seemed pleased. Mr. Raghu Ram asked Hari questions regarding his education and other matters. However, Mr. Sankar Rao interjected, sharing the troubling revelation that Hari hadn't visited school or uttered a word for the past two years. Concerned, Mr. Sankar Rao sought the assistance of a revered Swami Ji and a local herbalist, both of whom reassured him that Hari was physically well. Nevertheless, the silence persisted.

In the muted depths, Saru's voice pierced through the air, breaking the muffled and obscured atmosphere. With a tone of concern and support, she shared a peculiar tale about a childhood friend who had experienced a sudden transformation.

Once, an energetic and vibrant friend of hers had inexplicably withdrawn from social activities, attended irregular schooling, avoided friends, and communicated only when absolutely necessary for survival.

Concerned about her sudden, alarming change, her parents embarked on a desperate search for answers. They sought the counsel of numerous doctors, but each visit yielded the same baffling response: physically, there was nothing wrong with her. Determined to find a solution, they continued their quest, ultimately finding a doctor whose expertise hinted at a potential cause. This doctor speculated that perhaps she had encountered a horrifying incident, one that had instilled a profound fear within her. As a result, she may have chosen to silence herself as a means of self preservation or she could have been coerced into silence by a menacing incident.

With a renewed sense of hope, the parents made arrangements for her to see the doctor for counseling. It was during these sessions that she gradually began to unravel the tightly wound threads of her distress.

In a courageous moment of vulnerability, she shared the truth that lay dormant within her. She had indeed witnessed a harrowing event, an occurrence so traumatic that it had stifled her voice and imprisoned her emotions. But now, with the help of counseling and support, she has managed to find solace and reclaim her voice.

As Saru's words hung in the air, heavy with both relief and intrigue, an unexpected noise shattered the stillness. A kettle crashed to the ground, its deafening clang resonating through the room. Startled, everyone in the vicinity snapped to attention, their concern palpable.

Sanjay, sensing the urgency, rose from his seat and swiftly made his way to the kitchen, his footsteps echoing against the tiled floor. Meanwhile, Ravi, the elder son of Mr. Shankar Rao, seized by an explicable restlessness, furiously rummaged through the shelves of cupboards, his hands frantically shifting through the contents. His actions were laden with purpose, as if he were searching for something he had kept earlier.

Sanjay: Oh, it's you, Ravi; how are you? What are you doing? I inquired about you. You didn't come to meet me?

Ravi: Hi Sanjay, I just returned from the neighboring town, where I had some important unfinished tasks to complete. I was actually on my way to meet you, Sanjay.

Sanjay: Ravi, that is fine, but why are you treating me so formally? And you appear to be under stress; is everything okay? Did you engage in any messy activities?

Ravi: Sanjay, I am fine; I am just tired from the trip. It is all good, I assure you.

Sanjay: All right, come on, let me introduce the other members.

Sanjay and Ravi strolled together, hand in hand, as they made their way towards the enchanting dining hall. Sanjay, donning a look of excitement, introduced Ravi to the gathered people at the table, emphasizing their deep bond as close friends. With a sparkle in his eye, Sanjay regaled everyone with stories of their exhilarating adventures and thrilling treks during their visits to the farmhouse. He extolled Ravi's remarkable skills with vehicles, hinting at the hidden depths of knowledge he possessed about every nook and cranny of the village.

As Sanjay spoke, an air of happiness enveloped the gathering, and the others warmly engaged with Ravi, eager to hear more about his experiences and expertise. Laughter filled the room, and despite the lively conversations, Mr. Raghu Ram, known for his enigmatic nature, remained mysteriously quiet, observing the interactions with a curious smile playing on his lips.

After everyone had finished their meal, everyone cleared out, but Saru remained seated in the dining hall. Hari, who had been in the kitchen, returned carrying a plastic tub and a cleaning cloth. He began collecting the plates one by one, but as he did so, Saru stood up from her chair and gathered the plates closest to her side of the table. She handed them to Hari with a comforting smile and an attempt to have a talk with him. Hari took the plates and placed them in the tub, but instead of fully clearing and cleaning the table, he went abruptly inside the kitchen. Unperturbed, Saru decided to leave the dining hall as well. As she walked and climbed the stairs towards her room, she unexpectedly encountered Mr. Raghu Ram on the staircase.

Saru: Hi uncle, to which floor? Why don't you use the elevator inside?

Mr. Raghu Ram: Saru, to reach the top floor, open space for some fresh air and a beautiful mini garden, as suggested by Mr. Sankar Rao.

Saru: Oh, then let me join you.

Mr. Raghu Ram: Sure.

Saru and Mr. Raghu Ram ascended to the top floor. Raghu Ram's mobile phone buzzed; he searched and picked a corner of the open space to talk over the phone. Saru discovered a captivating open space that beckoned her to immerse herself in the beauty of nature. A gentle breeze caressed her face, and to her delight, a magnificent garden adorned the space, brimming with an abundance of seasonal and ornamental plants, creating a picturesque scene that seemed straight out of a botanical wonderland. Saru found herself drawn to a cozy seating area nestled amidst the verdant surroundings.

After finishing the call, Mr. Raghu Ram joined Saru.

Mr. Raghu Ram: Too beautiful; someone must have invested the hours for this output.

Saru: Appreciable work, and uncle, if you don't mind, can I ask you something?

Mr. Raghu Ram: It's about the murderer of Sanjay's parents. if I am not wrong.

Saru: Absolutely yes. Where me and Rishi struck, there was so much work to do, and we lied to the parents about this sudden trip to here.

Mr. Raghu Ram: I am in that job. I will find him in one or two days, and you both will forget about everything and have a peaceful time here.

Saru: Hmm, we both should come out clear, and I feel pity for Sanjay but not for what he has done to us.

Mr. Raghu Ram: No worries, dear.

While Saru and Mr. Raghu Ram continued to chat, they sensed someone was coming. When Saru moved from the place to see Hari, He walked to the small room at the corner, which was locked, and got the keys from his shorts pocket and took care to open it. He picked up the gardening kit and other things to do some digging and watering.

Saru walked to him and offered for help; he initially denied it, but after insisting, he handed over the watering pipe to her to water the plants. After some time, Saru saw Mr. Raghu Ram go, and she continued to water plants. As she finished, she saw Hari doing potting mixing for new samples.

Saru: Do you mind? If I join you. Let me tell you about my recent plant-saving adventure. Instead of a garden of flowers for my birthday, I received a nursery of potted plants with names that are as difficult to pronounce as tongue twisters, and it's like plants come with their very own secret language. I was really excited and decided to take on the responsibility of caring for these plants myself, completely overlooking and ignoring all the tips and advice given by our gardener. One by one, these precious little plants started witting away, as if they were participating in some twisting game of dying fast. It was like a race to the bottom, and I didn't want the score to hit zero. I made a wide decision by handing over the charge of my dying green buddies to our gardener. Phee! I felt like a superwoman, swooping in just in time to save the day and increase the oxygen levels in our little corner of the world.

Hari burst into laughter; the sound filled the surroundings, showing all the teeth in the arches and being reminiscent of someone being tickled relentlessly. He handed Saru a pair of rubber gloves and patiently demonstrated to her the art of mixing the ingredients, the intricacies of potting, and the techniques of watering the plants. They spent a considerable amount of time together.

Mr. Shankar Rao came to them, and he was surprised to see a smile and a happy face on Hari.

Mr. Shankar Rao: Rishi was in search of you; you had left your mobile in the dining hall. I noticed you walking up the stairs with Raghu Ram, sir. Everyone seems to be gearing up for a trip to the apple and strawberry farms.

Saru: Thank you for informing me about Rishi's search for me. Hari, would you like to join us on this mini trip to apple and berry farms? I believe that your unique perspective and creative style would be a remarkable addition to the experience.

Hari wore a joyful expression on his face as he received Saru's invitation, clearly revealing his happiness. However, in an instant, his facial expressions changed to a mixture of confusion and concern. Mr. Shankar Rao, perceiving this shift, quickly left the place, assuming that Hari might decline the invitation if he were present. Sensing Shankar Rao's understanding, Saru made an effort to persuade Hari to accept the invitation, but he denied it. Saru respected his decision and waved him goodbye.

Saru made her preparations and met Rishi. She proceeded to recount her recent encounter with Hari, providing Rishi with a detailed explanation like a kid giving an explanation to his mother after a picnic.

Rishi: Oh, that's cool; if you inquire about the car accident, I am certain he must have some details to share. It's worth approaching him with empathy and sensitivity, which can help create a promising environment for discussing such a sensitive topic.

Saru: Well, I am thinking the same, but I missed a good opportunity as he denied coming with us.

Rishi: Fingers crossed! It's time to hit the road; I reckon everyone must have hopped into the vehicle by now.

After reaching the vehicle, Saru and Rishi spotted that all the seats were occupied, as if the long awaited Best of the

Annual Day Show was about to kick off. To their wonder, they noticed another parked vehicle adjacent to the Toyota. Inside that vehicle, Mr. Raghu Ram took a seat behind the wheel while Hari occupied the passenger seat beside him. Instantly, Saru and Rishi instinctively joined Hari in the vehicle without pausing to contemplate their decision.

The engines of both vehicles roared and hit the road. Hari, occupying the front seat, reached into his environmentally friendly cloth bag and retrieved a box, which he quickly handed over to Saru. Filled with curiosity, Saru accepted the box without hesitation and eagerly opened it. To her delight, the box revealed fritters made with pan leaves.

Everyone's excitement soared as the tantalizing aroma of the fritters wafted through the air. Unable to resist any longer, they picked one up, taking in its enticing aroma before taking a satisfying bite. Saru couldn't help but share their unfamiliar and newly discovered delight with others, passing the fritters around for everyone to enjoy.

Saru: Hari, you are a multifaceted person. You are a plant buddy and also have culinary expertise, and from what I have heard, you study well and aspire to start your own business. You are also a good friend.

Rishi: Certainly, Saru. Why not restart your studies, Hari? I believe you have one more year of school to attend, after which you can enroll in a city college with support from Saru and me.

Saru: Brilliant! I never thought of this before, but that is okay. What Rishi says, I say. What do you think, Hari?

Rishi: I observe Hari remaining silent and even appearing unimpressed by our suggestion, Saru. If this suggestion does not work out for you, we may be able to find another program where you could continue your education.

Saru: Hari, feel free to speak your mind. We can all agree that you are in a secure and safe environment where you can express yourself without worrying that someone else in the vehicle will hurt you or judge you.

Hari: cried and shouted, Yes...! It pains me to say that I have a burning desire to study, and it weighs heavily on my heart to see my father in need of care, and it's my utmost priority to provide for him.

After hearing and witnessing Hari's words, Mr. Raghu Ram stopped the vehicle safely beside the road, avoiding the obstruction to the flow of traffic. Rishi and Saru envisioned his outburst impending, and they kept to themselves, giving importance to Hari's words.

Mr. Raghu Ram: Hmm, Hari. I totally know that you are in a stable state both mentally and physically, but it's evident that something is burdening and bothering you. I am a police officer, and we are all here to help and protect you.

Upon discovering that Mr. Raghu Ram was a police officer, Hari's fear and tension escalated exponentially. The realization of Mr. Raghu Ram's profession left Hari apprehensive and on edge. On the other hand, Saru and Rishi found themselves caught in a state of confusion, and the unexpected revelation created a sense of bewilderment for them.

Hari: Police... I do not know, and I did not see anything.

Saru: Calm down, Hari; he is my uncle.

As Hari stood there, beads of sweat trickled down his forehead, his palms turned wet, and his body trembled uncontrollably. His sudden transformation caught the attention of Saru and Rishi, who exchanged concerned glances. Mr. Raghu Ram, who was seated in the driving seat, swiftly stepped out and motioned for everyone to join him.

Reluctantly, they followed Mr. Raghu Ram's urgent gesture and stepped out of the car. The sight that awaited them was both awe-inspiring and treacherous. Mammoth rocks of uneven sizes and shapes lined the side of the road, creating a precarious path that led to the daunting valley. The sheer drop was enough to send shivers down their spines; any misstep could result in crushed bones and a fatal fall.

As they cautiously made their way onto the rocky terrain, the tension in the air grew palpable. But it was Hari's reaction that had Saru and Rishi stumped. Fearful, he burst into tears, resembling a lost child in desperate need of comfort and reassurance. His distress heightened the suspense, leaving both Saru and Rishi utterly perplexed.

Without hesitation, Mr. Raghu Ram swiftly reached into his pocket and retrieved a handkerchief. Gently, he handed it to Hari, offering him a small respite from his anguish. Leading Hari to a nearby rock, he guided him to sit down and grasped his trembling hand firmly, an anchor of support amidst the unsettling surroundings. Rishi and Saru stood motionless at the required spots to watch Hari and Mr. Raghu Ram.

The mystery deepened as they remained in this precarious location, with no immediate understanding of why Hari had become so emotionally unhinged.

Mr. Raghu Ram: Does something knock you down by looking at this place?

Hari: Please, I do not know anything, Sir. Drop me off at the farmhouse.

Mr. Raghu Ram: Well, I will. Only if you open your mouth and let the secrets spill from the depths of your mind.

Hari: I know nothing.

Mr. Raghu Ram: Again, I am assuring you that you are in safe hands. I am a very good human being; don't compel me to act like a cop now.

Hari: Yes, I witnessed the incident, which resulted in the demise of Sanjay's parents, which turned my life upside down and also left Sanjay alone. It happened a few years ago when they came to visit, unknowingly making it their last visit. Sanjay's parents were incredibly kind and caring. They provided us with more than enough support and took care of our family's expenses. However, my father's earnings were sufficient to meet our basic needs and sustain our lives. Unfortunately, my brother became entangled in bad habits and surrounded himself with the wrong friends. Daily fights became commonplace in our home, and things worsened after the demise of my mother. He stopped providing money to my father openly and started taking it secretly. Consequently, things began disappearing from the farmhouse.

One day, my father caught Ravi red-handed. When my father questioned him about it, a huge argument erupted. He pushed my father away, and Sanjay's father witnessed the altercation and attempted to intervene. However, he disregarded any pleas to stop. As a result, Sanjay's father pushed him, causing him to fall onto the sharp edge of a sofa and sustain an unintentional injury. This act actually saved my father from further harm.

Filled with rage, Ravi left the house in a fit of burning anger and did not return that night. Both my father and I were worried sick about him. He remained out of reach until the following night, when he unexpectedly showed up at home, clearly in a distressed state. He smelled of cigars and alcohol, had a tired face with red eyes, and blabbed by looking straight at me as he walked into his room.

Mr. Raghu Ram: Hmm, okay, what happened next?

Hari: As I walked into the room to check on him, I found him fast asleep. With Sanjay's parents at the farmhouse, my dad generally stays behind to attend to any needs that might arise during the night. Since my father wasn't feeling well, I decided to stay at the farmhouse as well and arranged to sleep in the hall.

That night, I struggled to fall asleep as unsettling and incomprehensible images plagued my dreams. Startled awake, I sat up and noticed a peculiar noise emanating from the kitchen. The room was shrouded in darkness, but I illuminated my way with the light from the mobile's torch. As I cautiously made my way towards the kitchen, I caught sight of Ravi leaving through the back door. Acting quickly, I closed the door behind him and followed in pursuit.

I walked in silence, with him a few steps behind and me trailing close behind. Eventually, he stopped near the edge of a valley—the same valley we find ourselves in now. He positioned himself beneath a tree, directly across from the gaping darkness of the abyss. Something about his gaze into the void filled me with a sense of dread.

Unbeknownst to him, I stood there, lurking quietly, waiting, and trying to comprehend the situation. Exhaustion eventually overtook me, and I fell into an uneasy sleep. The first rays of daylight pierced through the mountains, rousing me from my slumber. It was then that I noticed Sanjay's parents' car parked near the edge of the valley. Assuming they had arrived, I started heading towards them, intending to offer my greetings. However, just as I began to move, an enormous car seemingly materialized out of nowhere and forcefully pushed Sanjay's parents' vehicle over the edge, hurtling it into the depths of the valley.

My body trembled uncontrollably, leaving me paralyzed with fear. As I directed my gaze towards the person emerging from the car, a profound sense of unexplainable trepidation swept over me; it took my breath away. Before me stood Ravi, the person with whom I shared not only parental bonds but also life's journey, and the very same person who had cold-heartedly and mercilessly killed Sanjay's parents, executing a calculated plan. Regrettably, our eyes met, a connection that sent a shiver down my spine, making me fall to the ground.

Later, as news of the incident spread, the police arrived to investigate. Witnessing the aftermath, Ravi's anxious expression made it clear that he was feared. The incident left me bewildered and filled with an unshakable sense of dread. The mysterious events of that fateful morning would haunt me, and as the investigation unfolded, I couldn't help but wonder about the sinister forces at play and the true nature of the person I had followed into the darkness.

Mr. Raghu Ram didn't speak much and recorded everything and said, Well, you opened up everything. Hari, don't worry; I will take care of everything, and don't bring about any change in your behavior. Saru and Rishi were in shock after realizing the truth behind the tragedy. All of them got back into the vehicle and reached the farm. By then, another vehicle was parked, and all of them were already at the strawberry farm.

Observing Sanjay and Ravi's camaraderie while exploring the farms, Saru and Rishi found themselves overwhelmed by inexplicable emotions. They couldn't understand how Ravi could maintain a normal and friendly demeanor towards someone who was in immense pain and also responsible for the distressing situation they were all facing.

After spending some time visiting different viewpoints and covering the farm, the group eventually made their way back to the farmhouse.

The next morning, as everyone gathered for breakfast, an atmosphere of tension lingered in the air, especially for Hari. Rishi and Saru remained silent, their minds consumed with curiosity about the actions Mr. Raghu Ram would take now that he knew the identity of the murderer.

The room fell into an eerie silence as everyone savored their food without uttering a word. Suddenly, Ravi materialized, his presence casting a shadow over the atmosphere. He motioned for Sanjay to join him, a silent command that carried an air of urgency. Sanjay, however, instinctively denied the request, urging Ravi to join him for breakfast instead. Displaying impeccable manners, Ravi gracefully accepted the invitation, pulling out the chair opposite Sanjay.

Meanwhile, Mr. Raghu Ram, Who had been seated at the table, rose to his feet and swiftly cleared the remnants of his meal. With a purposeful stride, he made his way toward the entrance. At that moment, a group of armed policemen entered the hall, their stern expressions and weapons creating an unsettling tension. The occupants remained frozen, unable to make a single movement.

The environment was suspenseful, and Hari, who had been standing nearby, made a subtle gesture towards Saru. Ravi's senses sharpened, a feeling of apprehension coursing through his blood stream. Sensing danger, he attempted to stand up, his eyes fixed on Hari.

Before Ravi could react, Mr. Raghu Ram interrupted, his voice dripping with disdain. He wanted Ravi not to be clever, expressing his discontent with Ravi's intelligence, which had been on display for far too long. Without further ado, Mr. Raghu Ram coldly aimed his gun at Ravi and shouted,

Just a little moment, I will fire a bullet directly into the body. The room erupted into chaos and confusion.

Mr. Shankar Rao's trembling hands folded together as anguish and terror flooded his expression. "My Ravi, he whimpered, his voice laced with pain and fear. He may have been mischievous and indulged in vices, but please don't hurt him." Tears streamed down his face as he desperately tried to come to terms with the unimaginable. The revelation that Ravi, his son, could be associated with such a heinous act sent shockwaves through his entire being.

Mr. Shankar Rao's heart wrenched as he contemplated the possibility that he had failed to recognize the true depths of his son's character. As the tears continued to flow, he clung desperately to the hope that there must be an explanation, a hidden truth, that would absolve Ravi of this grave accusation. His grief stricken plea echoed through the air, carrying the weight of a father's shattered trust.

Amidst the cacophony of conflicting voices echoing in every direction, Ravi defied the chaos and focused his attention solely on Mr. Raghu Ram. Ignoring the words hurled his way, he summoned an immense reserve of courage and determination. With a sudden surge of energy, he forcefully pushed the chair aside, creating a physical barrier between himself and his adversaries. Ravi took a back step and retreated, his movements deliberate and calculated. As he distanced himself from the commotion, his eyes locked on Sindhu.

In a swift gesture, Ravi reached out and firmly clasped her hand and made a powerful and threatening statement, declaring that anyone who dared approach them would face the full force of his fury.

The room descended into a state of pandemonium. Gasps of astonishment and disbelief filled the air as onlookers struggled to comprehend the scene unfolding before them. Sanjay in particular was in a state of intense shock as the truth about Ravi's darker and crueler side began to sink in. The realization that his trusted friend harbored such a menacing capacity sent shivers down his spine, forcing him to confront the unsettling truth about the depths of Ravi's character.

ACP: Ravi, this is the final warning; don't hurt her and surrender.

Ravi: I don't want to spend my life in prison; I will not leave until I make my exit.

As Ravi and Mr. Raghu Ram engaged in a tense exchange of words, an air of unease settled over the onlookers, each one silently regretting their inaction towards helping Sindhu. Ravi's firm grip on her neck caused Sindhu great pain, intensifying the gravity of the situation. Sensing an opportunity, Ravi carefully calculated his escape plan, intending to slip away unnoticed through the kitchen's backdoor.

Mr. Raghu Ram, well-versed in covert communication, discreetly signaled to a fellow officer, instructing him to cover the kitchen's backdoor.

With a subtle motion of his left hand concealed behind his body, Mr. Raghu Ram conveyed the urgent message.

Behind the scenes, a hidden officer relayed the information to another colleague stationed just outside the entrance door, positioned in such a way that he remained invisible to anyone inside. The message swiftly passed through the ranks until it reached the officer closest to the kitchen's exterior door.

The officer, determined and alert, received the crucial message and wasted no time. With practiced precision, he pushed the door open slightly, careful not to create any unnecessary noise. Concealing a firearm at his back, he confronted Ravi, demanding the immediate release of Sindhu. Ravi, realizing the gravity of the situation and the threat posed by the gun, hesitantly loosened his grip on Sindhu, who fled to the safety of Sanjay's arms, reminiscent of a lamb escaping the jaws of a ferocious tiger.

The atmosphere crackled with tension as other officers swiftly moved forward, surrounding Ravi like a swarm of insects descending upon a helpless moth. Overwhelmed and outnumbered, Ravi had no choice but to succumb to their authority. He was quickly taken into custody, and his freedom was abruptly extinguished like a dying flame. The collective sigh of relief from the onlookers mingled with the palpable sense of justice prevailing in the room as Sindhu's tormentor was finally brought to justice.

After a brief silence, Mr. Raghu Ram entered the hall and approached Shankar Rao, placing a hand on his shoulder. Sanjay and Sindhu, still stunned, observed Mr. Raghu Ram's presence, and Sanjay walked to him.

Sanjay: I reflect upon the heart-wrenching events that unfolded when my parents tragically lost their lives. Sadly, I was not present at the time, as I found myself in Italy, separated by distance and unaware of the impending tragedy. It took me a painstaking two days to finally reach the location of the incident, filled with anguish and sorrow.

Upon my arrival, the police informed me that my parents' passing was deemed an accident. However, my close friend Ravi vehemently disagreed, revealing that it was not a mere accident but rather the result of inebriated individuals who carelessly crashed into their vehicle during the early hours of the morning.

Overwhelmed by grief and struggling to come to terms with this devastating truth, I made a firm decision to take matters into my own hands and embark on a personal search to unveil the identity of the person responsible for my parents' untimely demise. As I delved deeper into the investigation, a shocking revelation emerged: the person behind this tragedy was none other than Rishi. Initially, disbelief consumed me, making it arduous to accept such a painful reality. Nevertheless, the unbearable pain I endured pushed me to confront and inflict harm on both Rishi and Saraswati, driven by my unwavering determination to seek justice for my beloved parents.

Mr. Raghu Ram: Hmm, everything will be fine. That day, when Rishi and Saru were also in the nearby valley, Ravi saw them and observed their moves. They visited the valley every day, and he made up a story. When the police took time to investigate, what if they got to know it was a planned accident? To clean his hands, he narrated a fake story and gave you the wrong information, and he would be successful in convincing you. I am so sorry the police didn't see what really happened. Their lives were tragically cut short when their car careened off the road and plunged into a deep valley, where the lack of oxygen proved fatal.

The situation was made worse by the fact that the car was completely buried under several feet of mud and was engulfed in a landslide. Ravi dismantled the vehicle he used so as to leave no trace.

Sanjay, without saying a word to Mr. Raghu Ram or anyone else present in the hall, left for his room, and Sindhu followed him quietly. Without much saying or sharing, everyone else emptied the hall.

After a rather eventful day, the next morning arrived. The group had gathered their luggage and was eager to embark on their journey to their homes even before breakfast time. As they assembled, they realized that Mr. Shankar Rao and Hari were nowhere to be found. Concerned, Sanjay decided to take matters into his own hands and walked towards Mr. Shankar Roa's shack. He approached the door and knocked gently, waiting for a response. The door creaked open, revealing Hari standing there with a sorrowful expression on his face.

Hari: Dad is sleeping, and he is not well.

Sanjay entered the house, his footsteps rousing Mr. Shankar Rao from his slumber. Visibly shaken, he stood on his feet.

Mr. Shankar Rao: Sorry, Sanjay, I was sick and couldn't make you breakfast, but by lunch time I will be ready.

Sanjay reached into his trouser pocket and extracted a folded, bulging envelope, extending it towards Mr. Shankar Rao. Surprise filled his eyes as he accepted the envelope and unraveled its contents, revealing a stack of cash. However, after a brief moment, Mr. Sankar Rao returned the envelope to Sanjay, declining the gesture, and spoke with a sense of gratitude, acknowledging that Sanjay had already done more than enough for his family. He humbly expressed his inability to accept the money. Sanjay forced him to take it, and he bid a farewell and said he would visit soon.

As everyone entered the city, it was already lunchtime. Mr. Raghu Ram decided to disembark before entering the city and told the driver to drop them all off at their respective homes. As the vehicle approached its final stop, the sight that greeted them left the entire family standing outside with expressions mirroring a drought stricken landscape that had endured months without rain. Rishi and Saru were taken aback; their surprise was evident as they witnessed the unexpected gathering of their family members eagerly awaiting their arrival.

Rishi and Saru stood in front of their parents.

Rishi: We are sorry.

Mr. Mukesh: Don't be Rishi; we are all so proud of you both, and Raghu told us everything.

Saru: about?

Mrs.Sharmila: We know what has happened in the past few days and how you both tackled everything without our help.

Mrs.Roja: Yes, I am so proud of you both, but you both should have informed us earlier; we would understand and respect your decisions, especially you, Rishi.

Mrs.Srinivas: Yes, Rishi, when you don't want to marry Sindhu, that's fine, and we're all ok with it.

Mrs. Roja: I knew from the beginning that you were not happy with the proposal of marriage with Sindhu. But I am not talking with you; you lied to me when I asked you about marriage.

Rishi: Ha ha, you are my sweet and smart mom; you get everything as if it's written on my face.

After a burst of mixed emotions, everyone walked into the house. Mrs. Roja said, Rishi, you are going to marry the Girl that was suggested by me, and no more drama. Hearing this, everyone paused. Mrs.Roja responded, I meant his and everyone's. The room is filled with laughter.

Rishi and Saru eased back into their routine after a brief but refreshing break with the family. The family embarked on their week-long adventure, which they had chosen to spend on one of the most renowned private islands.

Epilogue: Ties That Bind

As the final lines of "Unveiling Bonds: Journeys of Love, Truth, and Family" fade away, we're left to ponder the twists and turns of fate, the resilience of love, and the deep connections that tie us all.

Time has flown since those pivotal moments that brought the family back into the warm embrace of understanding. Rishi and Saru, once grappling with uncertainties, now stand united, their eyes fixed on the future, having matured through their shared tribulations. Their love, like an old wine, has deepened, revealing richer notes as years rolled by.

The unbreakable bond between Mr. Shankar Rao and Sanjay tells a tale of friendship that has weathered storms and basked in sunlit moments of joy. That old shack, which once whispered secrets and held pain, is now a beacon of shared stories and laughter. Their paths might have veered in different directions, but their shared past ensures that their lives are forever woven together.

The author, the true puppet master behind this ensemble, subtly reveals her own heart's whispers through her characters. Her cherished garden, where life bursts in joyous green, mirrors the very relationships she has so lovingly portrayed.

And as this chapter ends, a realization dawns – life is but a collection of stories, of moments. The people we come to adore, the obstacles they navigate, and the wisdom they glean, they all linger, like gentle murmurs, long after their tales are told.

"Unveiling Bonds: Journeys of Love, Truth, and Family" serves not just as a story, but as a reflection on the myriad emotions we all navigate. It celebrates the choices we make, the ties we cherish, and the serendipities of fate. And as we bid adieu to this world the author crafted, we're left with a heart full of hope – that our own tales, like those of Rishi, Saru, and others, will be defined by love, grit, and the chase of true happiness.

May the essence of this story stay with you, a gentle reminder that every decision, every bond, every fleeting moment is a stitch in the quilt of your life. As you set this book down, know that the story of your life is still being written, with every heartbeat, every hope, every dream. And in your hands lies the pen to script your own beautiful saga.

www.ingramcontent.com/pod-product-compliance
Lightning Source LLC
LaVergne TN
LVHW091308150826
845673LV00006B/1583

* 9 7 9 8 8 9 0 6 7 9 4 5 1 *